Florence Marryat

A Crown of Shame

Vol. I

Florence Marryat

A Crown of Shame
Vol. I

ISBN/EAN: 9783337047719

Printed in Europe, USA, Canada, Australia, Japan

Cover: Foto ©Andreas Hilbeck / pixelio.de

More available books at **www.hansebooks.com**

A CROWN OF SHAME.

VOL. I.   *a*

A CROWN OF SHAME.

A NOVEL.

BY

FLORENCE MARRYAT,

AUTHOR OF

'LOVE'S CONFLICT,' 'MY SISTER THE ACTRESS,'
ETC. ETC.

IN THREE VOLUMES.

VOL. I.

LONDON:
F. V. WHITE & CO.,
31 SOUTHAMPTON STREET, STRAND, W.C.

1888.

EDINBURGH
COLSTON AND COMPANY
PRINTERS

CONTENTS.

———ρ———

								PAGE
CHAPTER I.	.	.	.	.	.	.	.	I
CHAPTER II.	.	.	.	.	.	.	.	29
CHAPTER III.	.		.	.	.	.	.	56
CHAPTER IV.			.	.	.	.	.	83
CHAPTER V.			.	.	.	.	.	110
CHAPTER VI.	.	.	.	.	.	.	.	139
CHAPTER VII.	.	.	.	.	.	.	.	166
CHAPTER VIII.	.	.	.	.	.	.	.	204

A CROWN OF SHAME.

A CROWN OF SHAME.

CHAPTER I.

IT was the close of the hot season in San Diego, and the thunderous clouds that hung over the island rendered the atmosphere still more oppressive. Liz, the Doctor's daughter, stood at the open door of their leaf-thatched bungalow, gazing out into the starless night, and wondering when the rain would come, to relieve the intense heat and disseminate the sickness that was so rapidly thinning the population. The stillness was so unbroken that one might almost be said to feel it. Not a breath of air stirred the light feathery branches of the bamboo, not even the chirp of a solitary insect could be distinguished from their covert in the long grass, nor a note from the songsters that crowded the surrounding woods. The trailing creepers that hung like a gorgeous eastern canopy of crimson and purple and orange from the roof of the verandah, brushed their blossoms against her face, as she thrust it into the night, but they brought no sense of refreshment with them. Liz felt stifled for want of air, as she withdrew from the verandah, and re-entered the bungalow, with a deep-drawn sigh. But the sigh was for others. She was not a woman to make otherwise than lightly of her own pain or inconvenience. To witness suffering or distress, and be unable to relieve it, that was the great drawback of life to Elizabeth Fellows. She was not a girl, and the existence she led had tended to make her older than her age. She was five-and-twenty, and ever since she was a little child she had been motherless, and brought up to depend upon herself, and to minister to others rather than be ministered to. Her father, Dr Fellows, was generally considered to be a reserved, morose, and rather disagreeable man : but Liz knew otherwise. She was his only child, and ever since she could remember they two had lived together, and alone, and he had been both mother and father to her. He was not lively and talkative, even to Liz—but she had always felt that he was unhappy, though something in his manner had forbidden her inquiring the cause of his reticence and melancholy. But he had never said an unkind word to her. Gravely and affectionately he had brought his daughter up to help him in his work, and Liz, who possessed an active, clever brain and a large amount of courage, had taken an immense interest in the science of medicine and surgery, and knew almost as much about it as himself. Dr Fellows left all the simple cases in his daughter's hands, and for a long time past she had been almost worshipped amongst the negro population of San Diego, as a species of white angel who came to their women and their children with healing in her hands. And both the Doctor and his daughter had had plenty of work to do during the last few months. Fever was reigning paramount in San Diego.

Both Europeans and natives had been falling around them like rotten sheep; and with the epidemic had come a murrain on the rice-fields and sugar-cane plantations, so that the people had to contend with starvation as well as disease; and awful rumours of mutiny and insurrection had commenced to make the residents and planters feel alarmed. Inside the Doctor's cottage were grouped some score of negresses, most of them with infants in their arms. Their work was over for the day, and this was the hour when they came to Liz to have their bottles refilled with medicines, and to show her what progress their wailing little ones had made.

As she stepped back amongst them, her face assumed an expression of pity and sympathy for their distress, that did indeed make her look like an angel of good-

ness. She was not a beautiful woman—
far from it—but it is not, as a rule, the
most beautiful faces that are the most
comforting to look upon in a time of diffi-
culty or danger.

Liz had a tall, well-developed figure,
which her plain print dress showed off
to perfection. Her skin was clear, and
soft, and white, and her abundant fair
hair was tucked smoothly away behind
her ears, and twisted into a knot at
the back of her head. Her grey eyes
beamed with a tender, kindly light, that
had no power to conceal her feelings,
and her firm, well-shaped mouth showed
firmness and decision. In fact, she was
a typical English woman, with rather a
majestic bearing about her, as if she
knew her power and rejoiced in it. But,
above all, she was a woman to love
and trust in,—one who would never tell

a lie nor betray a friend, and yet who, once convinced that her own trust had been betrayed, would stamp the image of the offender from her heart, if she died under the process. As the negresses caught sight of her again, they were startled to see the tears upon her cheeks, hardly believing they were shed for them.

'Missy feeling ill?' 'Missy like a little wine?' 'I go calling Massa to see Missy?'

'No! No! What are you talking about? I am as well as possible!' cried Liz, hastily brushing her tears away. 'I was only thinking.'

'Ah, Missy,' said one poor mother, regarding an attenuated morsel of humanity which lay just breathing and no more across her lap, 'I thinkin' my little Sambo never run about again!'

'Don't lose heart, Chrissie,' replied Liz, in her grave, sweet voice, as she knelt down and laid her hand on the baby's forehead. 'He is very weak, poor little fellow, but so long as he can eat, there is hope for him. I will change his medicine, and perhaps we shall have the rain by to-morrow. A few cool nights would set him up again.'

'Ah! Missy very good to say so, but we shall have plenty more weeks hot weather yet. Poor little Sambo under ground before the rain sets in.'

'And my poor girl can't stand no ways!' cried another; 'and Rosa's boy die this afternoon.'

'Oh, what can I do—what can I do for you all?' exclaimed Liz, with her hands to her head.

At this moment, the group in the Doctor's bungalow was augmented by a fresh arrival. This was Rosa, the yellow girl, who rushed in like a whirlwind, with her dead child in her arms. Liz had taken an interest in this girl, but it was one which Rosa strongly resented. Her child was born out of wedlock, and the gentle remonstrances on her conduct which the Doctor's daughter had urged upon her, had been taken by the uneducated creature as an insult rather than a kindness. Her poor little dead Carlo had been tended as carefully as any of Liz's other patients, but the bereaved mother chose to think it otherwise, as she burst in upon them.

'He is *dead!*' she cried frantically, as she almost flung the body upon the table. 'And now, perhaps you will be satisfied, Miss Lizzy. Now you will be glad to think there is one bastard child less on my massa's plantation, and that I have nothing

—nothing left to remind me of my lover who has sailed away to America.'

'Oh, Rosa! how can you so misjudge me?' said Liz, as she put one arm round the weeping girl.   But Rosa flung it off.

'It is true!' she exclaimed fiercely; 'you said he had better never have been born, and now you have taken no trouble to keep him in this world.   I suppose you thought it would be a right punishment for my sin.   But I hate you—and the punishment shall come back on your own head!   I hope I shall live to see the day when you shall weep as I weep, and have nothing left you but the burden of the shame.'

'Rosa, you are not yourself!   You do not know what you are saying,' replied Lizzy calmly.   'It is God Who has taken your baby to Himself, and neither I nor any one could have kept him here.   Try and think of it like that, Rosa. Think of little Carlo, happy and well for ever in the gardens of heaven, and you will not speak so wildly and bitterly again.'

'I shall! I shall!' cried the girl, in the same tone, as she seized the body again and strained it in her arms; 'and I shall never feel satisfied, Missy Liz, till you suffer as I have done.'

And with that she rushed out again into the darkness.

Liz leant against the table, and trembled. These were the things that had the power to upset her. To toil for these people early and late; to be at their beck and call whenever they chose to summons her; to lie awake at night thinking of the best means to relieve their trouble, and then to meet with ingratitude and reproaches. It did indeed seem hard!

But it did not make her voice less sweet whilst addressing the others. The room in which they were assembled was long and narrow—the only sitting-room in the bungalow — and furnished with severe simplicity. The matted floor, the cane chairs, and plain unvarnished table, all told of a life of labour rather than of luxury, and except for Liz Fellows' desk and workbox, and a few books which lay scattered about, it contained few traces of occupation. Yet it was the very absence of such things that proved the inmates of the cottage were too busy to think of much beyond their profession. A large cupboard, with a window in it, at the end of the apartment, served as a surgery, and there Liz soon turned to mix the febrifuges and tonics required by her patients. As she did so, she was greeted by a newcomer.

'Hullo! Miss Fellows, as busy as usual, I suppose, and no time even to bid a poor mariner welcome.'

Liz turned at the sound of the cheery voice, with her welcome ready in her eyes.

'Oh, Captain Norris! Are you back again already? When did you arrive?'

The stranger's face fell.

'*Back again already!* And I've been absent from San Diego for at least six months, and thinking they felt like six years! When did I arrive? Why, this evening! The "Trevelyan" dropped anchor exactly at six o'clock, and directly I could get away, I came up to see you.'

'It is very good of you, and my father will be delighted to see you. I expect him in every minute. Sit down, Captain Norris, whilst I mix the medicines for these poor women, who are anxious to get to their homes again, and then I will hear all your news.'

She looked so cool and collected as, having dismissed her patients, she drew a chair to the table and sat down beside him, that Captain Norris did not know where to begin. He was a fine handsome young man, with dark eyes and hair; the skipper of a merchant vessel, and every inch a sailor; and he was very much in love with Lizzie Fellows. He carried several neatly tied up parcels in his hands, but he was too nervous to allude to them at once.

'I am sorry to find you have fever in the island,' he said, by way of a commencement.

'Oh, it is terrible—a regular plague!' replied Lizzie; 'and though my father has worked early and late amongst the negroes, we have lost patients by the dozen. It is sickening to hear of the numbers of deaths, and to witness the trouble; — enough to break one's heart.'

'But you keep well?' he inquired anxiously.

'Oh, yes! Nothing ever ails me! I have too much to do, and no time to be ill. But I am very sad, and somewhat disheartened.'

'Mr Courtney must have experienced a great loss.'

'Yes! His plantation is sadly thinned, but the deaths have been chiefly amongst the children. Mr Courtney is very good to them, and spares no expense to provide them with comforts. It is no one's fault. It is the will of God, and we must wait patiently till He removes the scourge. But there is great distress, and even starvation, amongst the native population in other parts of the island, and some degree of insubordination.'

'And how is Mr Courtney's beautiful daughter?'

'Maraquita! She is not ill, but she has been very languid lately, which we attribute to the heat. But I have not seen so much of her during the last few months. I suppose she is too gay to have any time to spare for us.'

'And Henri de Courcelles! Is he still the overseer at Beauregard?' demanded Captain Norris, after a short pause.

Liz coloured.

'Yes! Why should he not be so? Mr Courtney has every trust and confidence in him.'

'So much the worse, I think, for Mr Courtney.'

She fired up directly.

'Captain Norris, you have no right to

make such an insinuation! What do you know against Monsieur de Courcelles? It is unworthy of you to try and set his friends against him, behind his back.'

'I am sorry if you think so, Miss Fellows; I hoped that you might not be so intimate with De Courcelles as you used to be. But let us talk of something else. How is your father?'

'Much the same as usual, Captain Norris. Father is never very lively, as you know. Sometimes I fancy this climate must disagree with him, he is so silent and depressed; but he has always been the same, and he strenuously denies any feeling of illness.'

'It is a dull life that you lead here with him, Liz.'

'Don't say that! A useful life can never be dull, and I have many pleasures beside.'

'But you would like to see a little more

of the world, would you not? You would like to visit your native country, England, and make the acquaintance of your relations?'

Liz looked at him wistfully.

'I don't think I should, at least under present circumstances. I am afraid the pain of leaving San Diego, and all those whom I have known from childhood, would out-balance the pleasure of seeing fresh people and places. I have known no other home than San Diego, Captain Norris, and I don't think I could bear to leave the—the plantation.'

He did not answer her, but commenced, somewhat nervously, to undo the packages he held. As their contents came to view, Liz saw spread before her on the table a handsome morocco desk, a photographic album, and a complete set of silver ornaments.

'Oh, how beautiful!' she could not help exclaiming.

'They are for you,' said her companion brusquely; 'I brought them from England expressly for you.'

'*For me!*' repeated Liz wonderingly. 'Oh, Captain Norris, how very good it is of you! Whatever made you think of *me?*'

He seized the hand which was feeling the soft texture of the desk.

'I do not know, I cannot tell you, but it is the truth, Liz, that wherever I am, I always think of you. All the time that I have been away, your face and the sound of your voice has haunted me, and prevented my being charmed by any other woman. I love you as I have never loved before—as I never shall love again, because I shall never meet another woman so worthy of my love and my esteem.'

'Oh, Captain Norris, pray don't talk to me like that! You are mistaken ; I am not the good woman you take me for.'

'I must talk, and you must hear me to the end, Liz! I wanted to say all this to you last time I was in San Diego, but a grave doubt prevented me. But now I have come back to find you free, and I cannot hold my tongue any longer. I am not a boy, to be uncertain of my feelings. I am a man and my own master, and making a sufficient income to keep you in comfort. Be my wife, Liz ; I won't ask you to marry in a hurry, but promise you will be my wife some day, and I will summon up all the patience I possess, and live on the hope of the future.'

'I cannot,' she said, in a low voice.

'You *cannot !*' he echoed ; 'and why ?'

'I don't think you should ask me. I

don't think you have the right to ask me. But it is impossible. I shall never be your wife.'

'Does any one stand between us?'

Liz was silent. She would not tell the truth, and she could not tell a lie. Captain Norris turned on her almost fiercely in his keen disappointment.

'There does,' he exclaimed. 'I know it, without your speaking, and I know who it is into the bargain,—the same man who drove me from San Diego last time without speaking,—Henri de Courcelles.'

'You have no right to make the assertion, without authority,' retorted Liz Fellows; 'but since you have done so, I will not stoop to deny it. You are right; I am engaged to be married to Monsieur de Courcelles, but the fact is not generally known, and so I trust you will respect my confidence.'

Hugh Norris dropped his head upon his hands.

'Engaged,' he murmured, 'really and truly engaged! My God! why did I not have the courage to speak before?'

His despair roused her compassion. She drew nearer, and laid her hand upon his shoulder.

'Indeed, it would have been of no use, dear friend,' she said gently; 'Henri and I have made up our minds upon this matter for some time past, and should have been married long ago, had his position been a little better assured.'

'Oh, of course, I stand no chance against him!' replied Captain Norris bitterly. 'Monsieur de Courcelles, with his handsome face, and dandy dress, galloping about the plantation on his switch-tailed mustang, must needs carry everything before him. But he is not true to you,

Liz, all the same — and sooner or later you will find it out. If he is engaged to be married to you, he is a scoundrel, for he spends half his time at the great house making love to the planter's pretty daughter.'

'How *dare* you say so?' cried Liz, springing from her chair, and standing before him with her face all aflame. 'What right have you to take away my lover's character before me?'

She had been too bashful to call him by that name before, but now that she heard him (as she thought) so cruelly maligned, she felt he needed the confession of her love for a protection against his slanderers.

'Don't be angry with me, Liz! don't be offended, but I feel I must tell you the truth, even at the risk of never speaking to you again. De Courcelles is not worthy of you. Every one sees it but yourself. His attentions to Maraquita Courtney are the common talk of the town, and I heard bets passing pretty freely this evening as to whether the planter would ever countenance his impudent pretentions to her hand.'

'It is not true,' repeated Liz, though her face had turned very pale ; 'but if it were, I know no reason why Mr Courtney should object to Henri as a son-in-law.'

'You are wilfully blind to the fact then that he has black blood in his veins.'

Liz flushed crimson.   How impossible it seems, under the most favourable circumstances, completely to overcome the natural prejudice against the mixture of blood ; but she was true to her colours.

'I know more about him than you can tell me, Captain Norris ! I know that his father was French and his mother a Spanish Creole.   But it makes no difference to me. If he were all black, he is the man *I love*, and I will not stand by quietly and hear him defamed.'

'Who defamed him, Miss Fellows? I merely stated the general opinion as to De Courcelles' chances of winning Miss Courtney, though whether he succeeds or not is a matter of the most perfect indifference to me. But with regard to yourself, it is a different matter. I may be strong enough to bear my own disappointment, but I will not see you throw your happiness away without making an effort to save you. Oh, Liz, my darling,' cried Hugh Norris, forgetting himself in his anxiety for her, 'throw this man over, for Heaven's sake, or you will rue it your whole life long!'

'Your advice has somewhat lost its effect from what preceded it,' replied Liz coldly, 'and I must request you to spare it me in the future, Captain Norris. I also am old enough to know my own mind, and my friends from my enemies. I am very sorry that you came here to-night—still more so that you should have presumed to speak as you have done. I should have liked to keep you as a friend, but you have made that impossible. Please to relieve me of your presence, and let me quit the room until you are gone.'

'Oh, I will go—sharp enough!' said Captain Norris, as he rose from his chair and walked towards the door. 'You shall not ask me to leave you twice, Liz.'

'Stay!' cried the girl impetuously. 'You have forgotten your presents. Take them with you.'

'Won't you even keep the poor things I have carried so far for you?' he asked her humbly.

'Keep them!' she echoed scornfully. 'Keep a reminder always before me of the man who maligned my dearest friend to me? What do you take me for? No! If you have any wish left that I should forget this evening, and the pain you have caused me, take your presents away with you.'

'You set me a humbling task,' said Hugh Norris, as he collected his despised gifts and repacked them in their papers. 'But I will obey you. I would rather throw them into the swamp, than leave them here to annoy you. Only remember, Liz, that *I love you*, and that when the day comes (as it *will* come) when your other lover forsakes you, I will prove what I say.'

He went then without another word, though as he turned his eyes towards her for a farewell look, Liz saw a misty light beaming in them, which did not make her feel as triumphant as she thought she should have done to have gained the victory over him.

She was still standing by the table where he had left her, feeling hot and cold by turns, as she pondered over the rumour he had repeated, when a hasty footstep passed over the threshold, and Henri de Courcelles stood before her.

CHAPTER II.

EFORE she turned her head to greet him, Liz knew *who* had entered the bungalow. The marvellous instinct of love made her *feel* his presence, before she perceived it, and this instinct, common to all human nature, was deeply engrafted in that of Liz Fellows. She had a heart that not only wound itself round that of those she loved but entered into it, and made its home there, and she loved Henri de Courcelles with all the strength and passion of which she was capable. Their attachment had commenced more than a year before, when she and her father had brought De Courcelles through a dangerous illness, and Liz had nursed him into convalescence with the tenderest care, and the young man had rewarded her devotion with a confession of love, which she believed to be as genuine as her own. Before he rose from his bed of sickness Henri de Courcelles had pledged himself to marry Liz Fellows, and at the time perhaps had honestly wished to do so. But there were obstacles in the way of an immediate union, and the engagement had never been publicly announced. Henri de Courcelles was a man whose personal appearance would have proved sufficient justification in most women's eyes for Liz's excessive love for him. From his French father he had inherited a strength of limb and muscle, and a symmetry of proportion, which is not common amongst tropical nations, whilst his beautiful Creole mother had given him her Spanish eyes and colouring, with a little trace—though too slight to be offensive —of her African blood. Taken altogether, Henri de Courcelles was a very handsome and athletic young fellow, and with an easy grace about his bearing and mode of expressing himself that made him very fascinating. That his visits to her father's bungalow had been shorter and less frequent of late had never struck Liz as remarkable until Captain Norris had drawn her attention to the probable reason.

She was not of a jealous temperament, and where we love and fear to lose, we will hatch up any excuse to lull our doubts to rest, sooner than wrong the creature on whom all our hopes are fixed. Besides, Liz was too busy a woman to spend her days sighing over an absent lover. When she was not mixing and dispensing medicines, or visiting her patients, or reading the medical works recommended by her father, she had her household affairs to look after, or needlework to do, and oftener longed for more time than for less. And De Courcelles was a busy man also. She would hardly have liked him if he had not been so. He was overseer on the coffee plantation of the rich planter Mr Courtney, on whose estate Dr Fellows lived, and had the complete control and *surveillance* of the negro population. It made Liz's heart grieve sometimes to hear the coolies complain of his harshness and severity. She did not believe in her heart that Henri *could* be unjust to any one and thought the negroes only wished to escape the punishments they had incurred—still she could not help wishing, with a sigh, that he had the power to control them without punishment. But of course *he* could not be in the wrong— not entirely, that is to say. As she recognised his footstep on the present occasion, and all the painful doubt she was experiencing fled like magic before the pleasure of his presence, any one with a knowledge of physiognomy could have read how the woman loved him. Her pale face flushed with expectation—her quiet eyes glowed with fire—her whole frame trembled in acknowledgment of the man's supremacy over her. But as he advanced to the centre of the room and she could discern his features, Liz started with concern.

'Henri! what is the matter? Are you ill?'

'Ill! No,' he answered pettishly, as he flung himself into a chair. 'You are so mixed up with your pills and potions, Liz, that you can never imagine any other cause for a man's moods than illness. I'm right enough. What should ail me?'

'Ah! this dreadful fever, Henri. Forgive me if I am nervous for the safety of you and all whom I love. It strikes down its victims like a plague, and its terrible rapidity frightens me. It makes one feel so helpless. Sometimes it takes but a few hours to carry off its victims. I have been at three deathbeds to-day. It is enough to make a woman tremble at the least symptom of illness in her own people. And the epidemic seems to be on the increase. Nothing that my father does seems to stop it.'

'Well, try and find some livelier topic of conversation, Liz, for mercy's sake. It's enough to give any fellow the blues to hear you talk. I wish to goodness you followed some other calling, or rather none at all ; but since it is unavoidable, spare me the nauseous details. I have enough worries of my own without discussing your professional difficulties.'

Her sympathy was roused at once.

'What worries, dear ? Tell me of them. Can I do nothing to help you out of them?'

He coloured slightly under his dark skin as he stretched himself and said,—

'Nothing—nothing. They are matters of a purely private nature. But you know how I detest the coloured people, Liz. It is sufficiently annoying to me to be employed amongst the brutes all day long, without having to listen to a story of their grievances when my work is over. I come here for rest, not to talk about niggers.'

'Yes, I know, Henri, and it makes me happy to hear you say that you expect to find rest with me. But if you saw them suffer as I do, you could not fail to feel for them. Have you been very busy lately?'

'Pretty well. Why do you ask?'

'Because it is a week since you have been at the cottage.'

'You must be mistaken. I have called here several times when you were out. There's no finding you at home now-a-days, Liz.'

'I have been very much occupied, I know,' she answered quietly, 'but not so much so as to make me forget that you have not been here, Henri.'

The remembrance of what Captain Norris had repeated to her recurred to her mind, and on the spur of the moment she determined to learn the truth.

'You have been a great deal at the White House, have you not?' she continued.

He flushed again, and turned uneasily

in his chair, so as to avoid the straight-
forward glance of her eyes.

'Why do you ask me that question? I
am at the White House every morning
with my employer. It is part of my business to go there.'

'I don't mean at Mr Courtney's office,
Henri. I meant that you are a great deal
with Mrs Courtney and Maraquita—at
least I have been told so.'

'I am much obliged to whoever was kind
enough to interest himself in my private
affairs. Am I indebted to your old flame
Captain Norris for spreading untruths about
me? I met him skulking round the bungalow as I came along this evening.'

'Captain Norris does not *skulk*,' replied
Liz quickly. 'He has no need to do so.
Neither is he a " flame " of mine, and you
ought to know me better than to say so,
Henri.'

'Well, it looks like it, when you take up the cudgels so warmly in his defence. However, we'll let that drop. What has he been telling you against me ?'

'Nothing—or at least nothing of his own accord. He only repeated the common rumour—that you are a great deal in the society of Maraquita, and that—that people are talking about it.'

She stood for a few moments after that, expecting to hear an indignant denial from his lips, but De Courcelles was silent.

'Henri,' she continued softly, turning a very pale face towards him, 'it is not *true?*'

'What is not true?' he inquired brusquely.

'That—that you are tired of me, and making love to Maraquita Courtney.'

'Of course it isn't true ; it's a d—d lie, and the next time I meet that Norris, I'll break every bone in his body for saying so.'

She was all penitence for having suspected his fidelity in a moment. She flung herself on her knees beside his chair, and threw one arm around his shoulders.

'Oh, Henri! forgive me for having repeated such a slander, but it hurt me so, I couldn't keep it to myself. But it was not Captain Norris's fault. He only told me what he had heard in the town. He did not think, perhaps, that it was of so much consequence to me. And I know that you *are* very intimate at the White House; more so even than I am.'

'Well, Mrs Courtney is very civil to me, and I can hardly refuse her hospitality, on the plea that I am engaged to be married, can I?'

'No! No! of course not. But still— though I am *sure* that you are true to me,' cried the woman, fighting against her own horrible suspicions (for why should you

have asked me to marry you, unless you
loved me?) still, Maraquita is very lovely,
and she *likes* you, Henri, I am certain
of that. No! don't interrupt me! Let
me say all I have to say to the end, and
then perhaps I shall forget it. You see,
dear, I — I am not beautiful (how I
wish, for *your* sake, that I were), and there
is nothing in me worthy of your affection,
except my love! And I have seen something of men in my lifetime, and I can
understand something of their temptations.
Quita has been a flirt from a little child.
Who should know it better than myself,
who have been like a sister to her from
her birth? I was only five years old
when my father brought me to live at
Beauregard, and Quita was not born
for two years after that. I remember so
well the first visit I paid to the White
House to see the wonderful new baby, and

how proud I was when old Jessica let me
hold her in my arms—'

'Stop!' exclaimed De Courcelles authoritatively. 'What has all this to do with
me? I have no interest in these details
about Miss Courtney's birth.'

'I only mentioned it to show you how
well I must know Maraquita's character.
We have grown up together, Henri, and
I can almost read her thoughts. She likes
you more than a friend, and when I heard
the rumours about you, I felt as if I could
have no chance against her.'

Henri de Courcelles had risen from his
seat during her last words, almost shaking
off her caressing hand in his impatience,
and stood beside her, white and angry.

'I will hear no more of this nonsense,'
he cried; 'I have told you already it is
a lie, and you insult me by repeating it.
Miss Courtney and I are nothing to each

other, and it will ruin me with my employer if this absurd report gains ground. I shall get kicked out of Beauregard for nothing at all, and then all chance of our marriage will be at an end, and I shall probably have to leave San Diego.'

'It will not gain ground through *my* means, and I am only too glad to know that it is not true,' replied Liz, rising to her feet also.

She would have liked him to have put his arms round her and assured her with a kiss it was all an error, but she was too proud to show the blank disappointment that crept over her. Henri had denied the scandal, and she was bound to believe him, but still she was not satisfied, though she could hardly have given a reason for it.

'Of course—of course—I *knew* it was not true,' she repeated, in a quivering voice, as she tried to persuade herself that all was right between them. ' For once you *promised* me—do you remember it, Henri ?—that if any one ever came between us, you would let me know, so that at anyrate I should retain your confidence, even if I lost your love.'

' You harp so much on the question of losing my love,' he replied angrily, ' that you make me think you have no further use for it.'

Liz looked bewildered.

' Oh ! what have I said to make you speak like that ?' she exclaimed. ' When have I let you think that I was weary of you — we who have agreed to pass our lives together ? Oh, Henri ! is it my fault ? Has this misunderstanding sprung from my apparent coldness ? If so—forgive me ! For indeed—*indeed*—' continued Liz earnestly—all her reticence vanishing before the fear of offending her lover, 'I am not cold. I have so much important work to do, and serious things to think of, that I am afraid sometimes to let my thoughts dwell too much on our affection, lest I should not keep my mind clear. But that is not indifference. It is too much love,' she said, in a faltering voice.

'I have never doubted your love,' replied De Courcelles, softened by the sound of her tearful voice, 'and I don't want you to doubt mine, and especially not to listen to tales that have no foundation, and are calculated to injure my reputation. Maraquita Courtney is nothing to me, and never has been, and never will be. You may take my word for that!'

'Will you swear it?' cried Liz eagerly.

He hesitated a moment, and then he said,—

'Yes, I swear it by the God Who made us both!'

The woman dropped down into her chair again, and burst into a flood of hysterical tears.

'Oh! I *felt* it! I *knew* it!' she exclaimed. 'I have been so happy in the possession of your love. I was sure that Heaven could not be so cruel as to take it away from me.'

The young man crossed over to her, and laid his hand upon her bent head.

'No! no!' he said soothingly. 'No one shall take it away. You are not like yourself to-night, Liz. Where is all your courage gone to? You, who can stand by quietly and see an operation performed, or a patient die, who are the coolest and most collected woman I have ever met with. Why! I don't *know* you in this new character.'

' I *have* no courage where you are concerned,' she answered passionately, as she
looked up and met the glance of his dark
eyes. ' You are my life, Henri, and everything that is best in me, would die without
you.'

He winced a little as she spoke, but he
professed to laugh at her vehemence.

' It will not be my fault if you are ever
put to the test, Liz. How often have I
told you that my life belongs to you, since,
without your skill and care, I should have
lost it. Come, kiss me, and forget what
has passed between us. It is all the fault
of that meddling fellow Norris. I wish he
had been farther before he made mischief
between us.'

' No one has the power to make mischief
between us,' said Liz, smiling through her
tears. ' I am quite happy again now, and
am only sorry my foolish jealousy should

have betrayed me into making such a
scene. And, to prove it, let us talk of
Quita, Henri. I was wanting to see you,
just to ask after her.'

' Can't we find some pleasanter topic of
conversation, Liz ? Besides, you know
more of Miss Courtney than I could tell
you.'

' No ! That is just where it is. I have
hardly seen anything of her since the fever
broke out. Father is not quite certain
whether it is contagious or not, and whilst
there is a doubt, he thinks it better I
should keep away from the White House.
But old Jessica says that Quita is not
looking at all well, and she is afraid there
is something serious the matter with her.'

De Courcelles fired up again directly.

' Curse the old fool ! What business
is it of hers how she looks ! It's this
infernal tittle - tattle from house to

house, that makes all the mischief in the world.'

'Oh, Henri! You forget Jessica was Quita's nurse. Why, she loves her like her own child, and she says she has been very depressed lately, and is often crying. What should make her cry, Henri? Has she any trouble?'

'Don't ask me! How should I know?' he answered roughly. 'Miss Courtney is not likely to confide her troubles to her father's overseer. But I see no difference in her.'

'Perhaps it is only Jessica's anxiety,' said Liz thoughtfully. 'But I am always dreaming of this fever, and Maraquita is too delicate to battle against it. I wish Mr Courtney would send her out of the island until it is dispersed.'

'You don't think of going yourself, though.'

'*I!* Oh, dear no! I *should* be a coward to run away from these poor people when I can be of use to them. But Maraquita is different. She has nothing to do but to think of the trouble and brood over it, and she is easily alarmed. She would be much better away.'

'I suppose if her parents thought so they would send her. They have sufficient money to do anything. But we have discussed the subject enough, Liz, and I am weary of it. Where is your father?'

'Here he is,' replied Liz, in a brisk and cheerful tone, as Dr Fellows entered the bungalow.

Whatever her own doubts and imaginings, she was always cheerful before her father, for he seemed to carry a weight through life that would break him down, unless sustained by his daughter's strength of mind.

Dr Fellows was a man of about fifty years of age, but he looked older. His figure was bent and attenuated, his hair nearly white, his features lined with care and yellow from ill-health. No one to see them together could have believed him to be the father of the healthy and finely-formed young woman who advanced to meet him. The frank, ingenuous expression on his daughter's face contrasted pleasantly with his reserved and somewhat morose physiognomy. He hardly smiled as she took his broad-brimmed Panama hat and stick from him, and kissed him on the forehead. The doctor was dressed in a complete suit of white nankeen, and his face was scarcely less white than his clothes.

'You look very tired, father!' exclaimed

Liz. 'Have you been far from the plan-tation to-night, and are there any fresh cases?'

'I walked to the other side of Shanty Hill, to see a child of Mathy Jones, but I was too late. The fever had set in with convulsions, and it was dead before I arrived. And poor old Ben is gone too, Liz; Mr Latham's faithful old servant. I would have given all I am worth to save him, but I failed to do so. I think my right hand must have lost its cun-ning,' said the Doctor, in a tone of deep depression.

'No, no! father! It is nothing of the sort. You are overtired with your con-stant work, or you would not think of such nonsense. Let me mix you a white wine sherbet, you seem quite exhausted. And here is Henri, so talk of something else, and divert your thoughts.'

'How are you, Monsieur de Courcelles ?
We have not seen much of you lately,'
said Dr Fellows languidly.

The indifference with which he spoke,
showed that he did not care much for his
intended son-in-law.   Indeed, excepting
that he believed his daughter to possess
a much clearer and more practical head
than his own, he never would have sanc-
tioned the engagement.   But Lizzie loved
him, so the Doctor argued—and believed
in him, and therefore it must be all right.
Lizzie was too sensible to make a mistake
about it.   The Doctor forgot, or was
ignorant of the fact, that the cleverest
women often make the greatest fools of
themselves where their hearts are concerned, and their vivid imaginations make
them believe those they love to be all
they could wish them.   The handsome,
nonchalant young Frenchman did not

appear much better pleased to meet Dr Fellows than he did to see him, but he considered it worth his while to refute his assertion.

'That has been your fault more than mine,' he replied airily. 'I was just telling your daughter that I have made several attempts to find you at home, without success. My time is not my own, you know, any more than yours.'

'Oh, if Liz is satisfied, I am sure *I* am!' retorted Dr Fellows.

'It is all right, father, Henri and I perfectly understand each other,' interposed his daughter cheerfully. 'But had you not better go and lie down, father? I don't like that heavy look in your eyes; and you may be called up again at any hour of the night. Do take some rest whilst you can.'

'You are right, my dear,' replied the Doctor, staggering to his feet; 'I really want rest. But you will go to bed, too, Lizzie. You will not sit up too late with Monsieur de Courcelles ? '

'There is no fear of that, for I am going at once,' said the young man, as he rose to his feet. 'Good-night, Doctor ; good-night, Liz. I shall look in upon you again to-morrow.'

He nodded to each of them as he passed out into the night air, and Liz looked after his handsome lithe figure, as it disappeared behind the clump of mango trees, with a sigh of love and regret. But there was nothing but affectionate solicitude patent in her manner as she proffered her arm to support her father to his room.

'Father, you are trembling like a leaf. I think I shall give you a little quinine. By the way, have you heard any news from the White House to-day ? Are they all well ? '

' I trust so. I have heard nothing to the contrary ; and I saw Mr Courtney as usual this morning. What makes you ask me, my dear ?'

' Because Jessica said that Maraquita looked ill.'

' It can be nothing serious, or I should have heard of it. Probably the effects of this intense heat, and the unhealthy state of the atmosphere. But they are well provided with disinfectants at the White House, and Mr Courtney will not permit his wife or daughter to enter the plantation. They always drive on the other side of the island.'

' That accounts for my not having seen either of them for so long,' said Lizzie, as she left her father to lie down, dressed as he was, and try to gain a much-needed repose.

CHAPTER III.

AS she re-entered the sitting-room, she passed at once to the entrance which led on to the verandah. All the windows were wide open, and the shaded lamp upon the table, round which myriads of insects were hovering, conveyed no heat to the apartment, yet it seemed to stifle her for want of air. Her head and her heart seemed both on fire, and she could recall nothing of the events of the evening, except that Henri had denied he was untrue to her, and yet had left without giving her any proof of his fidelity. The world seemed to be crumbling beneath her feet as she stepped out of the open door, and lifted up her face to the star-spangled sky. How calm and peaceful and steadfast it appeared! What a contrast to her own turbulent spirit, and how she longed to be at peace also— anywhere, anyhow, only *at peace !*

Liz was passing through the cruellest phase of a disappointment in love—when merciless doubt obtrudes its fang into the heart, and poisons the whole being. How we despise and hate ourselves for doubt- ing, and yet how painfully we go into the minutiæ of our loathsome suspicion, and dissect every reason that forbids our cast- ing it from us!

Liz felt as if she dared not think about it. As she recalled De Courcelles' words and manner that evening, she saw that he had not said or done a single thing calcu- lated to set her mind at rest. Except the solemn oath which he had sworn, and somehow, though she loved him, Liz derived no comfort from remembering that oath, and even wished he had not taken it. That he might not have deserted her for the sake of Maraquita Courtney was true—as he had attested it, she was bound to believe it was true—but he was changed to herself. All the oaths sworn under heaven could not disabuse her mind of *that* idea ; and if he were false, what did it signify to her *who* occupied the place which she had lost ? The brave woman who could set a broken limb, or lance an abscess without wincing, shook like an aspen leaf at the prospect of losing her handsome lover. Her love was so knit to him, that she believed she could never disentangle it, but would have to live on, with her live warm heart beating against his dead cold one, until death came to release them. That is the worst of finding out the unworthiness of those whom we have believed in, — we cannot all at once tear our hearts away, and we despise ourselves for being so weak as to let them bleed to death by inches, instead of freeing them with one wrench.

Liz was ready to despise herself as she walked a little way from the bungalow. It stood in the centre of the coffee plantation, but a considerable space round it had been set with ornamental shrubs and trees. The glossy - leaved creamy - white magnolias, with their golden centres, shed their powerful perfume on the night air, and a clump of orange trees in full blossom mingled their scent with the magnolia. The night-blowing cistus and the trumpet flowers wound themselves up the supports of the verandah; the insects, with many a birr-r and whiz-z, disported themselves in the lemon grass, and from the covert of the plantation came low-toned murmurs from the sleepy love-birds, or the shrill cry of a green parrot startled from its bower of bud and blossom. Liz lifted her heated face to heaven, as though she would draw inspiration from its majestic calm.

Far off, from the cluster of negroes' huts, which bordered the property, she could distinguish the crooning wails of the mourners, preparing their dead for burial at sunrise, and her heart bled for the poor black mothers who had been compelled to part with the babies at their breast. Death and sorrow seemed to surround her, and her spirits sunk down to their lowest ebb. The stillness was intense. It was a night when one seemed lifted up from this lower earth, and capable of holding communion with the Unseen.

But absorbed as Liz Fellows was in her

own trouble, she was startled after a while by the sound of a low faint moan that came from the surrounding thicket. Her first idea was that it proceeded from Rosa mourning over her dead child— poor wild Rosa, who was so heedless as to be almost half-witted, and who had fallen a ready prey to some loafing young sailor who had spent a few days near the plantation. Liz had felt deeply interested in this girl. She had been shocked and horrified to find she had so little sense of decency or respect for her womanhood as to succumb to the first temptation offered her, but she had not slighted nor reproached the girl in consequence. Such things were common enough amongst the coolies. It was not Liz's vocation to preach but to console. She had indeed, whilst watching over Rosa and her baby, tried to convince her of the wrong she had committed, both to her child and herself, but the yellow girl had paid no attention to her words, until the fever had carried off little Carlo. Then they had come back upon her mind with double force, and she had resented them by insulting her benefactress. But Liz bore no malice. She was only anxious to console, as far as possible, the poor bereaved young mother, and when she heard the low moans, which she fancied came from Rosa, she plunged into the thicket whence they proceeded. She had gone but a few steps when she came upon a female figure leaning against the trunk of a mango tree, as though she had no strength to proceed further. But the first glance, even though given in the dusky light, showed Lizzie that this was no coolie girl — yellow, or otherwise. The slight form was enveloped in a black mantle, which covered it from head to foot, but the hood had fallen back, and in the white face turned up to the moonbeams, Liz recognised, to her dismay, the features of Maraquita Courtney.

' Quita!' she exclaimed, rushing forward, ' my dear Quita, are you ill ? '

But Maraquita shrunk from the kindly hand which was laid upon her, as if it had been the sting of a serpent.

' Don't touch me,' she murmured ; ' I could not bear it. I don't want *you.* I want—your—your—father.'

' My father is at home, dear. He will see you at once if you wish it. But why didn't you send for him, Maraquita, if you felt ill ? Why did you take the trouble to come down here to see him ? '

But all the answer Maraquita made

was to utter another heartrending moan as she swayed backwards and forwards with pain.

'Oh, my dearest girl, you are really ill! You must come to the bungalow at once, and let father prescribe for you. Lean on me, Maraquita, and let me support you. Only a few steps farther, and we shall be there.'

The girl she spoke to appeared to have no alternative but to accede to her request. She leaned heavily on Liz's arm, and with many a moan dragged her feet across the threshold of the Doctor's house, where she sank exhausted into a chair.

She was a beautiful creature, who had just attained her eighteenth year. Her fair-haired English father had imparted to her a skin of dazzling whiteness, with a complexion like the heart of a maiden-blush rose, and her Spanish mother had given her eyes dark as the sloe and soft as velvet, with languishing lids and curled lashes, and hair of rippling raven. Maraquita's form was slight and supple; her hands and feet small and childlike. She was in all points a great contrast to the Doctor's daughter, who regarded her as the loveliest girl she had ever seen. As little children they had been the most intimate companions and play-mates, Lizzie acting as an elder sister and protector to the little Maraquita, who toddled all over the plantation under her care. When older, too, they had studied together, or rather Liz had tried to impart the knowledge she derived from her father to Quita; but the latter had never advanced beyond the rudiments of learning. Her indolent, half-educated mother, who lounged about in a dressing-gown all day, and had no thoughts beyond her Sunday attire and her evening drive, considered schooling quite unnecessary for her beautiful little daughter, and much preferred to see her running about the White House in a lace frock and blue ribbons, with her rosy, dimpled feet bare, to letting her be cooped up in the bungalow studying grammar and geography.

So Maraquita had grown up to womanhood about as ignorant as it is possible for a young lady to be—about also as vain and foolish as it is possible for a woman to be. Yet Liz loved her—spite of it all—for the sake of those early memories. She had never relinquished her intimacy with Quita, and when they met, they were as familiar as of old, but they did not meet so often as before. The last two years, during which Miss

Courtney had been introduced to the
society of San Diego, had much separated
them. The pleasant evenings which they
had been used to spend together, wandering through the coffee plantation, were
gone for ever. Quita was always engaged
now, either to a dinner, or a ball, or to
go to the theatre with her friends, and
Liz had ceased to expect to see her.
And since the fever had broken out
amongst the coolies, they had never met,
and she was content, for Quita's sake, that
it should be so. And now to find her
wandering about the plantation at night
and evidently so ill, filled Liz's breast
with alarm. There was but one solution of the riddle. Quita had contracted
the fever in its worst form, and had come
to them in her delirium. Liz had no
time to do more than think the thought
before she deposited Quita in a chair and

rushed to wake her father, and summon him to her relief.

'Father,' she exclaimed hurriedly, as she roused Dr Fellows from his sleep, 'I am so sorry to disturb you, but it is absolutely necessary. Quita is ill—very ill, and you must come to her at once. I met her wandering about the grounds, evidently in great pain, and she says she wants to see you. I am afraid she is delirious. Oh, father, do come to her at once!'

'Maraquita *here?*' said the Doctor, as he rose from his bed and prepared to quit the room. 'And without her parents? Impossible.'

'Oh, father, I am sure she is not in her right senses, though she is too ill to speak much. What will Mr and Mrs Courtney say?'

'We must send word to them at once,'

exclaimed the Doctor, as he preceded his daughter to the sitting-room. But as soon as he had felt Maraquita's pulse, and listened to her moans, the expression of his face changed from concern to the deepest dismay. 'This is much worse than I anticipated,' he whispered to his daughter. 'We must carry her into my room at once.'

'Dr Fellows,' cried the sick girl, as she clutched at his coat sleeve, 'save me, for God's sake—save me! I came to you because you are so good and kind, but—but—I think I am dying.'

'No! No! my dear! it will be all right by - and - by,' replied the Doctor soothingly; 'but you must be good now, and do as I tell you, and you will soon be well. Liz and I are going to move you into my bedroom.'

'And shall I be alone with you?' she asked, with scared eyes.

'Yes!—*quite* alone! Now, Lizzie, take her feet, and I will carry her head and shoulders, and we'll have her on the bed in no time.'

'Is it the fever?' inquired Liz, with a white face, for she knew that Maraquita's constitution was very fragile.

'Yes! yes! Now, go and leave us, and tell this to no one.'

'But, father, let me undress her first.'

'I wish you to go at once and leave us alone,' repeated the Doctor firmly.

Liz obeyed her father's orders at once. She was too well used to work under him as an assistant, to dream of disputing them. But she was very much astonished to hear him send her away from her adopted sister's side.

'Shall I run up to the White House and tell Mr and Mrs Courtney that Quita is with us, father? They will be terribly alarmed if they find out she has gone.'

'Go nowhere, and speak to no one,' replied Dr Fellows authoritatively. 'They are *my orders*, remember. Remain in the sitting-room, and let no one enter the house. When I require you, I will call you.'

Liz walked out of the bed-chamber at once, and left her father with his patient. She could not understand him this evening, and his action alarmed as much as it puzzled her. Maraquita must indeed be ill, to make him look and speak with such complete dismay; he who was generally so cool and self-collected, and who appeared to look on death, whenever it occurred, as a kindly note of release from a

very troublesome world.   She drew out
her work (for whatever her mental perplexities, Liz was never idle) and sat
down to sew and practise patience.   She
could not help hearing the low moans
that forced their way through the wooden
partitions of the building, and her father's
soothing tones, but she could gain no
knowledge of what was passing there.
At last, after the space of an hour,
although it had seemed much longer, Dr
Fellows entered the room in which she
sat, and went to his cupboard in search
of some medicine.   His daughter looked
up anxiously as he appeared.

'Only tell me if she is better,' she
urged.

'She is not better yet,' replied her
father; 'but there is every hope she
soon will be.'

'Thank Heaven for it!   But I cannot help thinking of her poor parents. Perhaps they have discovered her absence, and are searching the island for her. It is cruel to keep them in suspense.'

'I think if you look at the matter from a sensible point of view, Liz, you will see that *when* they miss Maraquita, *my* bungalow is the first place they will visit. But I do not think they *will* miss her, at least not yet. Meanwhile I want to speak to you. Can you give me your serious attention?'

'Unless Quita should want you,' replied Liz, looking anxiously towards the bed-chamber.

'She will not do so for some little time, for I have given her a soothing draught, and she is asleep; and I can hear the least sound from where I stand. But it is necessary you should listen to me.'

' I am all attention, father.'

' You have spent the best part of your life in San Diego, Liz ; has it ever struck you as strange that I, an Englishman, and a certificated doctor, should have chosen to make my home in this island, and live, as it were, on the bounty of Edward Courtney?'

' I don't know that I have thought it *strange*, father, for you might have had a thousand reasons for settling in this beautiful island, but I have felt for a long time past that you have some secret trouble, to make you shun the curiosity or the publicity of the world.'

' You are right, Liz, and you are old enough now to share that sorrow—or rather that *shame*.'

' Oh! no, no, father, don't say *that !*' cried Lizzie, as her work dropped into her lap. 'Whatever it may be, it is not *shame.*'

'My dear, I cannot conceal the fact any longer, for without it you will never understand what I am about to tell you. The very name we bear, Liz, is not our own. I was compelled to adopt the name of Fellows, in order to escape—'

'WHAT? In Heaven's name, WHAT?' she exclaimed, clutching at his sleeve.

'*Transportation*,' replied Dr Fellows, in a low, strained voice.

She was about to scream out, to protest her horror of the disgrace attached to them,—her indignation that he should have brought it on their heads, — but a glance at her father's pale, pained face restrained her. In a moment she realised the awful effort it must have been for him to confess his guilt before his daughter, and womanly compassion took the place of her first resentment.

'My poor father,' she said, in a low voice, as she took his hands in hers. 'My *poor* father! Surely it was not deserved. There *must* have been some mistake.'

'No, Lizzie, there was no mistake. Since I have told you so far, you must hear all! I am a forger.'

She hid her face in her hands then, for she did not care to look at him, lest he should read the contempt she felt her features must express.

'This is the secret of the friendship between me and Mr Courtney. I owe him more than my life. We were boys at school together, Liz, and chums at college, and always the best of friends. But he was rich—the only son of a wealthy planter—and I was very poor, and had nothing to depend on but my wits. He led me into extravagances which I was too ready to follow, but whilst he had the means to defray his debts, I had no power to do the same by mine. At last, in an evil moment, to prevent a bill coming upon my old father which would have broken up his humble home and sent him to the workhouse, I forged my friend Edward Courtney's name, as a temporary relief. Before I could make up the money, the paper fell into his hands, and he might have ruined me; instead of which, Liz, he forgave me freely; but the rumour had got abroad, and I was a ruined man. I was married, and set up in a small practice. I lost it all, and it preyed so on your poor mother's mind that when you were born, she faded out of life, and left me alone with my disgrace. I took you away from

the place, and tried to establish a practice in various parts of England without
success—the whispered scandal followed
me everywhere—until Mr Courtney came
into his father's property, and settled out
in San Diego; then he wrote and begged
me for the sake of our old friendship, to
let the past be forgotten between us, and
to come out here and hold an appoint-
ment on Beauregard as medical overseer
to the plantation. As soon as I could
bring down my pride to accept a benefit
from the man I had so deeply wronged,
I brought you over here, and we have
been dependants on Edward Courtney's
bounty ever since. Lizzie, what do we
owe the man who has placed us under
such an obligation?'

'Our lives, should he require them,' she
answered, in a low voice.

She was deeply humiliated by what she

had heard. She had never dreamt that the evident trouble under which her father laboured could be the brand of shame. Her proud independent spirit writhed under the knowledge that she had been reared on the bread of charity,—that the very name she passed by was not her own, and that the best spirit which she and her father could claim from their benefactor, was one of tolerance only. She could have cried out to Dr Fellows then and there, to take her away from the surroundings which had become hateful to her, because they must evermore be associated with the bitter story of his guilt. But she only hung her head, and spoke in a whisper. Her father had been sufficiently degraded by having to tell her such a story, and he had been very good to her, and it was not his daughter's part to add to his suffering. But she threw the full depth of its meaning into the answer she returned him, and he caught at it eagerly.

'You are right, Liz. Our lives, and all we have, should be at his disposal, in return for all his goodness to us. You cannot feel that more deeply than I do. And now I want to hear you take a solemn oath to that effect.'

'*An oath!*' cried Lizzie, startled at the idea.

'Yes! an oath before Almighty God. Nothing short of it will satisfy me, and set my mind at rest.'

'Ah, father!' she exclaimed, remembering another oath which she had heard that evening, 'will not my promise do as well? You know that I would not dare to break it. It would be as sacred to me as any oath.'

'No, Lizzie—no! I am not asking this

for myself, but for another — for my friend Edward Courtney, to whom we owe so much, and nothing short of an oath will do. Say, " I swear before Almighty God, and by all my hopes of salvation, that I will never repeat what I may see, or hear, or suspect this night." '

' Oh, father! you frighten me! What terrible thing is going to happen?'

' Are you a child, to be scared by a few words? If you will not swear it, Lizzie, I will send you out of the bungalow this minute, to the house of our next neighbours, and you shall not return until I fetch you. But I want your assistance, and if you will do as I require you, you can stay and help me.'

' For Quita's sake then, father, " I swear before Almighty God, and by all my hopes of salvation, that I will never

repeat what I may see, or hear, or suspect this night." '

'That is my brave, good daughter,'
said the Doctor, as he laid his hand
for a moment on her head, before he
gathered up the medicines he had
selected, and left the room.

CHAPTER IV.

IZ stood where he had left her, awestruck and bewildered. All her private trouble of that evening—the sickening doubts she had conceived of her lover's fidelity, and her fears for Maraquita's safety—faded before the humbling truths she had just heard. *This*, then, was the solution of the riddle which had so long puzzled her—the meaning of her father's secret anxiety and depression. He was a criminal, whose crime was known to the law, and who had only escaped justice by yielding up his birth-right and hiding on the plantation of his benefactor, Mr Courtney. It was a *very* bitter truth to swallow.

Liz wondered how much Mrs Courtney and Maraquita knew of their disgrace, and what revulsion of feeling it might not cause in the breast of Henri de Courcelles. The thought of her lover caused a sharp pang to Lizzie. What terrible thing was about to happen in the future for her with regard to him? Her father's revelation had raised a new barrier between them—one which honour compelled her to feel could never be surmounted until she was permitted to reveal it; and what consequences might not follow such a confession. As Liz pondered on the difficulties in her path, she shivered to hear the keening of the night breeze as it sighed through the branches of the coffee trees, and the far-off wailing which could occasionally be heard from the negroes' huts. They seemed like a requiem over the ashes of her love and blighted hope.

The tears were standing on her cheeks when she was roused from her reverie by the opening of the door, and her father stood before her again.

' Do you want me ? ' she said quickly.

Dr Fellows answered her in a tone of portentous gravity,—

'Yes, Liz, though not in the way you imagine. Set your mind at rest concerning Maraquita. There is nothing to be alarmed at about her. But you must execute a commission at once for me. You must carry this basket to Mammy Lila on the Shanty Hill.'

Liz glanced at the large basket which

her father carried in his hand, with astonishment.

'I am to go to the Shanty Hill to-night, father? Do you know that it is five miles away, and it is just two o'clock? Cannot it wait until the morning?'

'If it could have waited till the morning I should not have told you to take it now,' replied the Doctor sternly. 'Have you already forgotten your own acknowledgment that we owe (if necessary) our very lives to Edward Courtney.'

'But what has this to do with Mr Courtney?'

'Ask no questions, but do as I bid you. If any one else could do the work as well as yourself, I should not trouble you, Liz. But I can trust no one but you. Carry the basket to Mammy Lila's hut, and leave it there. Tell her it comes from me, and my message to her is "*Silence and secrecy.*"'

'I will go,' said Lizzie shortly, as she took the basket from her father's hand.

'Go by the path that skirts the outer plantation, and cross the ravine by Dorrian's glen; it is the shorter way,' continued Dr Fellows; and then suddenly twisting his daughter round so as to look into her face, he asked her,—'Have you any fear? It is dangerous traversing these roads by night, and alone. There may be snakes across the path, or panthers lurking in the thickets. Are you sure you are not afraid?'

The contemptuous curl of Liz's lip showed him the futility of the question.

'*Afraid!*' she echoed. 'When have you ever known me afraid yet? Besides, if this is to be done for *Mr Courtney*, my life is at his service.'

'More than your life, Lizzie—your sacred
honour. Remember your oath, never to
reveal what you may hear, see, or suspect
this night.'

' I have not forgotten it,' said his
daughter briefly, as she threw a mantle
over her shoulders, and left the cottage
with her burden.

It was with strange feelings that she
set out to accomplish her errand. The
tropical night could hardly be called dark,
for the deep blue firmament was set with
myriads of stars, but the dusky glens
and leafy coverts were full of shadows,
sufficient to mask the unexpected spring
of wild cat or panther, or to conceal the
poisonous asp wriggling through the grass
on which she trod.

Yet she went bravely on, her only
means of defence a stout stick with
which she stirred the leaves in her

path, in order to unearth a hidden enemy.

The covered basket she bore was rather heavy, and she had no knowledge what it contained. Most women would have asked the question before they started— many would have untied and opened it as soon as they were out of sight. Liz did neither. A horrible suspicion had entered her mind, which she was fighting against with all her might, and it left no room for idle curiosity. On the contrary, she dreaded lest some accident should reveal the contents of the basket to her. She did not wish to ascertain them. She felt intuitively that the knowledge would be the cause of fresh unhappiness. So she walked rapidly and without a pause to Shanty Hill, though the five miles seemed very long without the landmarks familiar to her by daylight, and her feet were very weary before she got there.

Mammy Lila was an old negress who had acquired some repute as a herbalist, and was much sought after by the Coolie population to doctor their children. She was the *sage-femme* of Beauregard, and had helped Liz on many an occasion to usher the poor little dusky mites of humanity into a world which waited to welcome them with stripes and hard work. Mammy Lila was a seer into the bargain, and expectant brides and mothers were wont to go to her to read what fortune lay in the future for them. She was an old woman now, and rather infirm, but Dr Fellows had faith in her good sense and discretion, as he evinced on this occasion. The immediate approach to her hut was up a steep bit of hill, covered with loose stones, and as Lizzie, weary with mental and physical fatigue, toiled up it, she stumbled against an obstacle in her path, and shook the basket in her hand, from which issued in another second the feeble wailing cry of a new-born infant. Liz almost dropped the basket in her surprise. She had feared it, but she had resolved *not* to believe it, and now her worst suspicions were confirmed. She stood still for a moment, trembling at the discovery she had made, and then re-commenced almost to *run* up the rocky hill, as though she would run from the horror that assailed her. Panting with the exertions she had made, and almost speechless with dismay, she entered the negress's hut, white, scared, and hardly able to express herself. Mammy Lila was in bed, and had to be roused by repeated attacks upon her door, and when she answered the summons she was scarcely awake enough to understand what was said to her.

'Missy Liz!' she exclaimed in her surprise; 'who bad now? Not little Cora, sure! Dat chile not due for three week yet.'

'No, no, Mammy! I have not come for that,' said Lizzie, in a faint voice. 'The Doctor sent me. He said I was to give you *this*,' placing the basket on the floor, 'and to say his message to you is "*Silence and secrecy.*"'

'Ah! good Doctor know he can trust Mammy Lila,' replied the old negress, as she began to untie the basket lid. 'And what is this, Missy Liz — a baby?'

'I don't know—I don't want to know—don't ask me!' cried Liz Fellows, as she turned quickly away. 'Only remember father's message, "*Silence and secrecy,*"' and with that she ran quickly down the uneven rocky path again.

The loose stones rolled away from under her feet, and hurt them in her rapid descent, but she cared nothing at that moment for pain or inconvenience. All her desire was to get out of sight and out of hearing, and forget if possible the horrid task that had been imposed upon her. Maraquita—whom she had known from babyhood, and believed to be so innocent and pure, to have subjected herself to this penalty of shame. It seemed too awful and incredible a thought to be dwelt upon. Liz remembered, as she ran hurriedly homewards, how she had blamed poor heedless Rosa for the same fault,—how sternly she had reproved the ignorant yellow girl, who knew no better than to follow the instincts of her fallen nature, for her depravity, and told her she ought to have had more principle, and a better sense of right and wrong, than to yield to such a temptation. But Maraquita, so much beloved, so tenderly watched, so closely guarded, how could *she* have so deceived her friends and lowered herself; and *who* could have been so base as to lead her astray? This discovery, terribly as it affected Liz, cleared her lover's character at once in her eyes; and even in the midst of her pain, she could not help breathing a sigh of thankfulness to think that Henri de Courcelles was innocent of the charge imputed to him. He could never have been flirting with the planter's daughter whilst she had conceived a serious affection for some one else. Liz recalled the fervour of his oath with secret satisfaction; it was no wonder indeed that he felt justified in taking it, and she felt ashamed of the jealous spirit that had forced it from him.

But her thoughts soon reverted to her adopted sister, and she burned with resentment against her unknown betrayer. Her vow to Dr Fellows—which she felt to be as sacred as though uttered before God's throne ; the revelation which had been made to her that evening of their own disgrace ; pity for her friend's misfortune, and love for Henri de Courcelles, were all warring in her breast, and making her mind a chaos, as, wearied and panting, she stumbled over the threshold of her father's bungalow. She expected to find him alone with Quita,—to be able to tell him of her hopes and fears,—but, to her consternation, the room was full, and as she paused in the open doorway, her white and anxious face made her look like a guilty person. Mr and Mrs Courtney, with the old black nurse Jessica, were all there, and Dr Fellows was talking earnestly to them. As he caught sight of his daughter, he turned to meet her.

'*You know all*,' he whispered sternly, as he looked into her sad eyes, and squeezed her hand as in a vice. '*Remember your oath.*'

'Why, is that Lizzie?' exclaimed Mrs Courtney from the sofa, where she lay extended. 'I thought she was nursing our poor Quita. Whatever has she been doing out of doors at this time of night?'

'She has been to fetch me some necessary drugs,' replied the Doctor quickly.

Mrs Courtney had been a beautiful creature in her youth, but though not forty years of age, she had already lost all pretensions to good looks. She was corpulent and ungainly. Her large sleepy black eyes were sunk in a round face, with a yellow complexion, and triple chins. Her waving black hair was twisted untidily at the back of her head, and her abundant figure, unrestrained by belt or corset, was enveloped in a loose dressing-gown. But she rolled off the sofa nimbly enough when she heard the voice of Liz Fellows.

'Oh, Liz!' she exclaimed, grasping her hand, 'this is terrible news the Doctor has to give us; our darling Quita down with the fever. Fancy the dear child rambling to your house in her delirium! What a mercy she had sufficient sense left to guide her. She might have walked into the river. You may fancy what we felt when we heard that she was gone. Jessica found it out first when she went into her room with some iced sherbet, for Quita has been very restless at night lately. I suppose it was this horrid fever coming on, but she has been quite out of sorts for some weeks past. But oh! Lizzie, how *can* she have caught it?'

This long harangue had given Lizzie an opportunity to recover her equanimity, and she was able to reply quite calmly,—

'It is quite impossible to say, dear Mrs Courtney; but father does not think seriously of the case, and so you must not be too anxious about her.'

'But he will not let us even *look* at the dear child. Dr Fellows, I really think you are *too* particular. Surely her parents have the *right* to see her.'

'Certainly, my dear madam, if you insist upon it; but I think Mr Courtney will uphold my decision. I have not been able to determine if this fever which is decimating your plantation is contagious or not. I rather fancy it is epidemic, but it is impossible to say, because it is of no known character. It is surely more prudent, however, to keep on the right side. If Maraquita were in the slightest danger—if she were even seriously ill, I should be the first to entreat you to see her, but as it is, your presence would only do her harm. She is weak and exhausted, and everything depends on her gaining strength from sleep. Would you be so selfish as to excite and throw her back again, by disturbing her, or run the risk of contracting the disease yourself.'

' Certainly *not*,' interrupted Mr Courtney decisively. ' You are right, Fellows, as always are—'

('Don't say that,' interpolated the Doctor, in a pained voice.)

' —— and I forbid my wife going near the room where Maraquita lies. I can trust her to you, Fellows—implicitly, and with the most perfect confidence. I know you will do your very best for my dear child, and treat her as if she were your own.'

'Indeed—indeed I will, Courtney! If a sense of all I owe to you—'

'Hush! I will not hear you mention it. If such were ever the case, you have repaid it a thousand fold. And here I give you the best proof I could, of my friendship and affection. I leave with you my dearest possession — my only child. Fellows, my dear old chum, I know there is no need for me to recommend her to your care. You can remember how long it was before she came to us, how gladly I received the gift, and how precious it has been to me ever since. My very life is bound up in my little Quita. You will guard it—'

'With my own,' interrupted the Doctor solemnly. 'I would lay down my life to-morrow, Courtney, to save that of any one who is dear to you.'

' I believe it, my dear fellow, and, thank God, there is no necessity for such a sacrifice. You can assure us that Maraquita is in no danger.'

' On my word of honour, she is in no danger whatever, and in a few days she will be quite well again. All she needs is rest and quiet, and if you will trust her to Liz and me, we will see that she gets it.'

' We do trust her with you; and Liz, we know, will make the most devoted nurse,' said Mr Courtney, smiling; but as he caught sight of Lizzie's face, the smile faded. ' Holloa! what is this? Are you going to have the fever too? You are as white as a sheet.'

' It is the heat,' murmured Liz, in a low voice, as she turned away; ' and I have

had a great deal of nursing lately into
the bargain, Mr Courtney. Father and I
have the heartache all day long, to see
the ravages made by the fever amongst
the coolies.'

'Yes, it is sad enough,' said the planter,
'even for those who have not to count
the loss as I have, by pounds, shillings,
and pence. Do what we will to improve
the condition of these people, their natural
love of dirt and over feeding makes them
fall an easy prey to any disease. We are
quite sensible of what you and your father
have done for us, Lizzie. It is through
your means alone, that we have not lost
many more. You must not be disheartened on that account.'

'The distress seems universal,' continued Liz; 'the same floods that rotted
the vegetation, and caused this malarious
fever, have destroyed the rice fields, and

spread a famine amongst the negro population. The cases of starvation that reach
us every day are heartrending, because
it is so impossible to relieve them all.
Have there been any more riots in the
town, Mr Courtney ?'

'No, Liz. I have heard of none since
the military were called out to quell them.
But we must keep you up no longer. It
is already morning. Come, my dear Nita,
let us leave Dr Fellows and his daughter
to get some rest for themselves.'

But Mrs Courtney was still unwilling
to assent entirely to the Doctor's wishes.
She had no suspicion of the truth, but
she felt intuitively that something had
been kept back from them, and she was
curious to find out what it was.

'Let Jessica stay, at all events,' she
said; 'she has been Quita's nurse since
she was a baby, and has attended her

through all her illnesses. She will break her heart if you do not let her stay; and she can watch Maraquita when Lizzie is absent or engaged.'

'That sounds reasonable,' acquiesced Mr Courtney; 'and perhaps Jessica had better remain at the bungalow.'

But Dr Fellows was firm in resisting the proposal.

'Jessica can remain here if you desire it,' he answered, 'but she does not enter Quita's room. I am not even sure that Lizzie will do so. You have confided your daughter to my care, Mr Courtney, and you will not find me unworthy of the trust. I shall be both nurse and doctor to Maraquita, until I can bring her to the White House again.'

'You are a good fellow,' said Mr Courtney, wringing the Doctor's hand, 'and I do not limit the confidence I place in you. Jessica shall return with us, and we will leave Quita entirely in your care.'

'You shall have no cause to regret it,' replied Dr Fellows, as he accompanied them to the door of the bungalow. 'You can send down as often as you like for news of her, and I shall be found at my post, ready to report on her progress. But I honestly anticipate restoring her to you in a very short time.'

As he returned from seeing them off, and met his daughter's eye, his face changed, and his expression became very grave.

'That is well over,' he ejaculated, with a sigh, 'and the rest remains, Lizzie, with you and me.'

'Which means, father, that she is safe as far as *we* are concerned. Am I to go into her room?'

'No; I should prefer you should not. There is no necessity for your presence there, and I wish to leave you as unfettered as I possibly can. You have no notion how this calamity happened, Liz?'

'Not the slightest. I know so few of her friends. I have not even heard that she had an attachment for any one.'

'Well, it is a terrible business, but we must stand her friends, and see her through with it. She has told me nothing, poor child; but she has thrown herself upon my mercy, and entreated me to save her from the wrath and reproaches of her parents, and for their sakes I have promised to do so. She implores that even *you* shall not be told of her misfortune, and I have been obliged to humour her. We must keep up the deception of the fever, and as soon as she is sufficiently recovered to return home, the danger will be over.'

' But—Mammy Lila ! ' gasped Liz.

' Mammy Lila will do as I tell her, my dear, and at all risks this child's reputation must be saved. Everything else is an after consideration,' replied the Doctor, as he stumbled slightly, and saved himself by catching at the back of a chair.

' Father, are you ill ? ' cried Lizzie quickly, as she sprang to his assistance.

' No, I think not; but I will take a cordial, if you will mix it for me. I *must* not be ill until this business is settled, and Maraquita is safe under her parents' roof again.'

' But your hands are very cold, and you are trembling all over. Surely you are unfit for further work, and should go to bed and rest. Father, trust her to me. Don't overtax your strength, for her sake. You know that I am a careful and trustworthy nurse.'

'If I *die* in the effort, I will watch over her myself, and without assistance!' cried the Doctor excitedly, as he drank the draught she tendered him, and tottered back to the sleeping chamber.

Lizzie looked after him with the deepest anxiety.

'I am *sure* he is ill,' she said to herself, and if I am not very much mistaken, he has the symptoms of the fever strongly upon him. Oh, my poor father! is it possible that when you need the attention and skill you have bestowed on others, you will sacrifice yourself for the sake of this frail girl? Yes, I feel you will, even should it result in your own death. And I would have it so, though Heaven only knows what I should do without you— sooner than see you shrink from paying off one tithe of the heavy debt you owe to Maraquita's father. But the bearing of this heavy burden laid upon us ! Did Mr Courtney but know the weight of it, he would surely acknowledge his forbearance has not been in vain.'

CHAPTER V.

THE overseer of Beauregard occupied another bungalow on the plantation, a perfect bower of beauty, which, whilst lying close to the White House, was entirely concealed from observation by the glorious foliage that environed it. Its wooden walls were clothed in creepers, and surrounded by tall cocoa palms, and feathery bamboos and orange trees, with their double wealth of fruit and flower. The heavy perfumes by which the atmosphere was laden would have proved too much for any one but a man acclimatised to the West Indies, but they suited the sensuous, pleasure-loving nature of Henri de Courcelles perfectly. As he sat, or rather reclined, on a long bamboo lounge in his verandah, with a cigar between his lips, and his handsome eyes half closed, he looked the picture of lazy content. He was dressed in full white trousers, and a linen shirt, thrown open at the throat, round which a crimson silk neckerchief was carelessly knotted. His dark curling hair was thrown off his brow, and his olive complexion was flushed with the mid-day heat. His work was over for the time being, and he was free to rest and enjoy himself until the sun went down. He had been on horseback by six o'clock that morning, riding round the coffee and sugar plantations, keeping the coolies up to their work, and receiving the complaints of, or distributing his orders amongst, the men who worked under him. The labourers on Beauregard had long come to the conclusion that it was lost time to prefer any request out of the ordinary routine to Henri de Courcelles. Charming as he was when in the society of his equals, he was a stern and implacable overseer, being quick to find fault, and slow to extend forgiveness, and having no sympathy whatever with the people he ruled over. He looked upon the negroes as so many brute beasts out of which it was his duty to get as much work as possible, and he had often turned away with disgust on encountering Lizzie Fellows with a dusky baby on her lap, or with her arm beneath the head of a dying negress. He did not give vent to his

opinions in public. It would scarcely
have been safe, surrounded as he was
by the creatures he despised, and often
at their mercy; but they knew them,
all the same, and were ripe to seize the
first opportunity for revenge. Liz—with
her calm practical brain, and reflective
mind, should have seen for herself that
a man who could swear at an unoffend-
ing coolie, or thrust a little child roughly
from his path, or strike his horse between the ears with his hunting crop,
for no reason except to gratify a passing
temper, would never make a kind husband
or father. But the ancients never did
a wiser thing than to pourtray love
as blind. It blinds the cleverest of us
to mental as well as physical defects,
until some fatal day, the rose-coloured
glasses drop from our eyes, and we see
the man, or woman, love has idealised,

in their true colours. Liz saw some of
De Courcelles' faults, it is true, and grieved
over them, but there was always some
extenuating circumstance for them in
her love-blinded eyes ; and if there had
not been, it was only sufficient for her
lover to turn his glorious Spanish orbs
reproachfully on her, to bring her, meta-
phorically, to his feet. Well, after all, perhaps, if love were not foolish, and weak,
and blind, it would not be love at all,
but only prudence ; and the majority of
us would fare badly enough if *some one* did
not see us through rose-coloured glasses.
It would be terrible to stand before the
world as we really are, in all the hideous
nakedness of our evil tempers, and inclinations, and devices, and have no
sweet, generous, pitying, and all-believ-
ing love somewhere to throw a cloak
above our mortal nature, and believe

that the making of a saint lurks behind it.

Henri de Courcelles was thinking somewhat self-reproachfully of Liz that morning. The interview he had had with her the night before haunted him like a bitter taste when the draught is swallowed. He knew he had lied to her, and though the lie didn't trouble him, her complete belief in his sincerity did. If we tell an untruth, and it is fiercely combatted and denied by the opposing party, we are apt to tell a dozen more to uphold the first, until we almost swear ourselves into believing it. But if the falsehood is at once received as truth, and believed in with the most innocent faith, it makes us, if we have any feeling left whatever, doubly ashamed of ourselves. Henri de Courcelles had quite ceased to love Liz Fellows—indeed, it is doubtful if he had ever loved her at all—but he had admired and esteemed her, and these very feelings had killed those of a warmer nature. She was too good for him — too far above him. She humbled him every time she opened her mouth. Maraquita Courtney was a woman much more to his taste—sweet, ripe, youthful Maraquita, with her outspoken love and unbridled passion,—her red lips and wreathing white arms, and utter disregard of truth or principle. But Monsieur de Courcelles had not been easy about Maraquita lately. He was perplexed and anxious. He did not quite foresee how matters would turn out, nor what prospect lay in the future for them. He was somewhat ashamed of the duplicity of which he had been guilty to Liz Fellows, but he consoled himself with the idea that it had been forced upon him by his relations with Maraquita, and that it behoved him, as a man of honour, to divert suspicion from her, even at the risk of deceiving another woman.

As he was dreaming and ruminating on these things, he was surprised to see Mr Courtney approaching the bungalow. It was not the planter's custom to visit his overseer, and their business hours, which were usually passed in the office at the White House, were over for the day. De Courcelles sprang to his feet as his employer appeared, and proffered his seat for his acceptance. Mr Courtney sank into it without a word. He did not seem uneasy, but he was certainly unprepared to open the conversation. De Courcelles was the first to speak.

'I suppose you have come to speak

to me about Verney's grant, sir. I
should have given you the papers to
sign this morning, but as you were
not in the office, I brought them away
with me again. Will you see them
now ?'

'No, no! They can wait till to-
morrow,' replied Mr Courtney impatiently.
'Verney knows they are all right, and
the land is his. I was unable to attend
to business this morning, for I had a disturbed night, and slept late in consequence.'

'I am sorry to hear that, sir. What
disturbed you ?'

'The news has evidently not yet reached
you. Our poor Maraquita has been
dangerously ill.'

De Courcelles started, and changed
colour. His olive complexion turned to a
sickly yellow, and his brilliant eyes became dull and lustreless. The planter

was not blind to the emotion he expressed.

'Miss Courtney—ill?' stammered the overseer.

'Yes, very ill, and with this terrible fever. How she contracted it we are unable to discover, but she left her bed, and wandered in her delirium into the plantation, and fortunately towards the Doctor's bungalow, where she now lies. You may imagine what her mother and I felt when we heard she was missing. I thought Mrs Courtney would have gone distracted. However, the first thing I thought of was to ask for Dr Fellows' assistance, and luckily we found her there, but very, very ill.'

'She *is* better, I hope?' gasped De Courcelles.

'She *is* better, and, I thank God, out of danger,' replied Mr Courtney, looking him steadfastly in the face, 'and in a few days we hope to have her at the White House again. Lizzie Fellows, who has been like a sister to her, is nursing her with the greatest care. She is a most estimable young woman, clever, courageous, and thoroughly honest—good all round, in fact, and will prove a treasure to any man who is fortunate enough to win her. By the way, De Courcelles, I have heard a rumour that you are engaged to be married to Miss Fellows. Is it true?'

The overseer stammered still more.

'Yes—no—that is to say, sir, there *has* been some idea of such a thing between us, but nothing is definitely settled.'

Mr Courtney regarded the young man sternly.

'*Some idea!* Do you mean to tell me that you would presume to trifle with the girl, and hold out a prospect you have no intention of fulfilling ? Do you forget that she is the daughter of one of my oldest friends, and second only in my affections to my own child ? Dr Fellows is not the man to permit any one to play fast and loose with his daughter, and I should be as ready as himself to take up the cudgels in her behalf.'

' Indeed, sir, there is no necessity for such warmth on your part. You are judging me without a hearing. Lizzie and I perfectly understand each other. We are the best of friends, but at present I cannot see any prospect of our being more.'

' You mean to say that your salary is not sufficient to keep a wife upon ? '

' I have never looked on it in that light, Mr Courtney. Miss Fellows is devoted to her father and her profession, and we have hardly spoken of the time when she will be called upon to leave them.'

'Then you ought to have done so, Monsieur de Courcelles. A man has no right to make love to a girl unless he can talk of marriage to her. Now I have more than an ordinary interest in Liz Fellows, and if it is for her happiness to marry you, I am ready to further your plans. You need not wish to bring your wife to a prettier home than the one you now occupy; but I will engage to furnish it afresh, and double your present salary on the day you marry her. Will that bring matters between you to a crisis?'

Henri de Courcelles shifted his feet, and looked uncertain.

'I am not sure, sir; you see, you are precipitating them. Miss Fellows would be as astonished as I am, if she could overhear our present conversation. We have never spoken of marriage as a necessary contingency to our friendship.'

'Then you don't love the girl, and you don't intend to marry her?'

'I don't say that, Mr Courtney. It is impossible to say what we may decide upon in the future; but for the present, I positively deny that we have any fixed plans whatever.'

Mr Courtney looked dissatisfied for a moment, then, with the air of a man who has made up his mind to do a disagreeable thing, he proceeded,—

'Well! no one can settle these matters satisfactorily, but the parties concerned, and so I have no more to say about it. But there is another subject uppermost in my mind, which I feel I must mention to you. It is a delicate one, which I would much rather avoid, but I cannot shirk my duty. I have been unable to help observing, De Courcelles, that you admire my daughter Maraquita. I can hardly suppose you entertain any hopes from that quarter, but if you do, you must dismiss them at once, and for ever, for I have quite different views for Miss Courtney.'

The handsome young overseer had flushed dark crimson during his employer's speech, but he did not immediately reply to it.

'I hope I may be mistaken,' continued Mr Courtney, 'and I hope I have not offended you by mentioning it, but I have meant to do so for some time past. Maraquita is a lovely girl. I cannot help seeing that, though I am her father, and doubtless you appreciate her beauty, in common with many other men; but it can never go any further.'

'I have never presumed to think it could,' replied De Courcelles, with dry lips, and a husky voice.

'It is not *you* to whom I have an objection,' said the planter, 'it is to any man who cannot give Maraquita wealth and position. She is my only child, and I have great ambition for her; and I have already received a flattering proposal for her hand, from one of the highest men in the island. Had it not been for this unfortunate illness, I should have submitted his letter to my daughter by this time. But I have little doubt how she will receive it. Meanwhile, I think it but kind and just to let you know of my intentions, and to warn you, should there be any need of caution, to be careful.'

'I thank you, Mr Courtney, for your consideration,' replied De Courcelles, in the same hard dry voice, 'but there is no need of it. I hope I know my duty and my position too well, to aspire to

Miss Courtney's hand. No one can help admiring her, nor being grateful for any kindness she may extend to them, but there it ends. You have nothing to fear for me, nor I for my-self.'

' I am glad to hear you say so,' replied Mr Courtney, as he rose to go ; 'in a few days I expect that you will hear great news from the White House, and see preparations for a grand wedding, and then you will better understand my fears lest all should not prosper with my dear child, as I hope it may do. Meanwhile, do not forget what I said respecting Miss Fellows and yourself. If I can forward your happiness, you may count on my sympathy and assist-ance.'

And with these kindly offers of help upon his lips, Mr Courtney walked away, leaving Henri De Courcelles bewildered by what he had heard. Maraquita ill, and in the Doctor's bungalow, with her secret, perhaps, made patent to the world! And yet her father evidently knew nothing, and some one must have stood her friend, and shielded her from discovery. But Maraquita about to make a high marriage, and be lost to him for ever. That was a still more wonderful revelation, and one which he found it impossible to believe. Maraquita, who had so often sat, during their moonlight trysts, with her arms twined about his neck, and assured him that no man but himself should ever call her his wife. Henri de Courcelles would never have presumed, without a large amount of encouragement, to lift his eyes to his employer's daughter. He knew that his birth and his position would both preclude him as a suitor, in Mr Courtney's mind, and that it would be considered the height of presumption on his part to make proposals of marriage for her. But he had trusted to Maraquita's influence with her parents, eventually to gain their cause; he had trusted also to certain love passages which had taken place between them, to bind her effectually to himself. And now the announcement of these intended nuptials did not make him so unhappy on his own account as they alarmed him for their mutual safety. What might not Maraquita say or do, in her dismay at the prospect of being separated from him?

Henri de Courcelles secretly acknowledged his fickleness with regard to Liz Fellows, who had loved him well and constantly all along, and yet he could not believe that any one else could be unfaithful to him. The devil invents so many excuses for us wherewith to cover our own frailty, but they all disappear when we are called upon to judge our neighbour's sin. As soon as Mr Courtney had left him, Henri de Courcelles, feeling very uncomfortable under the close examination to which he had been subjected, resumed his cigar, and his lounging attitude, and lay for a long time pondering over the morning's interview. How much did the planter suspect, or know? Had his assumed warning been only a blind to entrap his overseer into an open confession, or surprise him into betraying himself? De Courcelles blessed his lucky stars that his self-control had not forsaken him, and that if Mr Courtney were on the lookout for a probable lover for his daughter, he had wrung no hint of the truth from him. But was the story of the fever true? That was a point on which he felt he must satisfy himself, and reaching down a wide Panama hat, he proceeded at once into the plantation. He looked handsome enough, as he strolled leisurely beneath the trees, towards the negro quarters, the fine plaited straw hat, which shaded his features, tipped jauntily to one side, and a red rose in the buttonhole of his white drill jacket. But his face looked perplexed and anxious, and he gnawed his moustache as he went. The negroes' huts were situated half a mile away from his bungalow, but they were close to that of Dr Fellows, and De Courcelles knew that in one place or the other he should find Lizzie, and hear the truth from her. But as he passed her cottage, he caught sight of her sitting at the window, sewing. Her face was pale, and her eyes red. She looked as if she had been both sitting up and weeping, though her print dress was fresh and dainty, and her glossy hair carefully arranged. A fear shot through the heart of Henri de Courcelles, as he drew near her, but the bright smile with which she welcomed his presence, drove it away.

'Why, Henri, what brings you here so early?' she asked, from the open casement.

'Didn't I say last night that you would see me again to-day?' he answered, as he took her hand.

'Yes, but it is hardly wise of you to walk about in the sun, unless there is a necessity for it.'

' You are right, Lizzie; but I am a messenger from Mrs Courtney; she sent me down for the last bulletin of her daughter.'

Lizzie looked surprised.

'How very strange! I sent up word by one of the servants half an hour ago!'

He felt then he had not lied quite so cleverly as usual, but he got out of it by saying,—

'The brute has probably taken a circuit of five miles, in order to attend to his own business. You know what these niggers are, Liz. However, give me the last news of Miss Courtney, and I will see it is delivered.'

Liz's face grew very grave.

'She is better, Henri. I have not seen her this morning, but my father tells me so, and that in a few days she will be quite well. I have just been making her some fish soup.'

'Was she very bad with the fever?' he asked.

'Very bad indeed. It is lucky I met her wandering about the plantation, or I don't know what might have happened. But there is no need for anxiety now. All danger is at an end.'

'Were you with her in her delirium? Did she—did she—*rave* much? I only ask for curiosity. I have heard that some of the negroes tried to destroy themselves during the fever; and her parents are very anxious still.'

'Are they?' said Liz carelessly. 'I thought my father had set their minds entirely at rest. As I said before, there is no occasion for it. Quita is quite sensible now, and only needs to regain her strength.'

Henri de Courcelles looked much relieved. He drew a long breath, and

straightened himself against the supports of the verandah.   Liz regarded
him for a moment, and then said, in a
low voice,—

'I want to tell you something, Henri.
I have been thinking over what I
mentioned to you yesterday, and I feel
I did you an injustice.   I can't tell you
how the conviction has been forced
upon me—but it is there.   Will you
forgive me for my causeless jealousy?
I have no excuse to offer for myself,
excepting that I love you, and I fear
to lose you.'

He only answered,—

'I told you plainly you were wrong!'

'I acknowledge it *now*, but *then*, I
thought only of what I had heard.   But
I see how foolish I was.   A long night
of reflection has shown it to me.   The
illnesses and troubles of our friends

are enough to make us think, Henri. *We* might be struck down to-morrow, and how doubly sad it would be to go whilst any misunderstanding existed between us and those whom we love.'

She spoke so plaintively that his feelings were touched on her behalf.

'There is something more the matter with you, I am afraid, Liz, than mere regret for such a trifle. Something worse than that must have happened to annoy you.'

'No, no!' she cried, in a voice of terror; 'nothing has happened, I assure you, Henri; but life is uncertain, and I may be sorry some day to think I ever misjudged you. Things are not always what they seem, you know, and unexpected barriers rise sometimes to foil the brightest hopes. Let us resolve to be patient with each other, so that

we may have nothing to reproach ourselves with if—if—anything should occur
to part us.'

The tears were standing in her patient
eyes as she raised them to his, and
the sight affected him. The man was
not wholly bad — none of us are — but
his senses drowned his better feelings.
He knew—even at that moment, when
his whole mind was fixed on Maraquita,
and full of fears for her safety — that
this woman was the more estimable of
the two, that she loved him the best,
and was the most worthy of love in
return. But his heart had gone astray-
ing, and he could not recall it at will.
He could only pat Liz's hand, and
profess to laugh at her fears, all the
while he knew how well founded they
were.

'Why, what should occur to part

us ?' he answered lightly ; ' unless, indeed, you elect to throw me over. But I thought we had settled that point satisfactorily last night, Liz ?'

' Oh, I was not thinking of *that !* ' she exclaimed hurriedly. ' It was quite another idea, and one of which there is no need to speak of to you now, for which, indeed, the necessity may never arise. But we shall always be *friends*, Henri—shall we not ? true and steadfast friends, whatever may occur ?'

' I don't understand you. You are speaking in enigmas to me,' he said petulantly, as he dropped the hand he had taken in his own.

They were indeed playing at cross-purposes — she, thinking only of the story her father had told her, and he of Maraquita and her possible revelations.

Liz sighed, and redirected her attention to her work. The same dissatisfied feeling which she had experienced the night before crept over her again, and turned her sick and cold, and it was not dispersed when Henri de Courcelles, after an awkward silence, lifted his broad-brimmed hat from his brow, and walked gloomily away.

CHAPTER VI.

 WEEK had passed away since Maraquita Courtney had entered the Doctor's bungalow, and the moment that Liz dreaded had arrived — they were to meet again. Never once had she entered Quita's chamber during the period of her illness. Dr Fellows had chosen the oldest, most stupid, and most deaf negress on the plantation to attend to his patient's wants, and sternly forbidden his daughter to enter her presence. But to-day she was

pronounced convalescent, or sufficiently
so to return to the White House,
and her parents, who were naturally
anxious to have her home again, had
arranged to fetch her away that afternoon.   Dr Fellows had said to his
daughter a moment before, on passing
through the sitting-room,—

'Maraquita is up and dressed, and
will be with you in a short time. She
is still weak and nervous.   Mind you
say nothing to upset her;' and Liz had
promised, feeling almost as nervous at
the idea of the coming interview as
Quita herself could have done.

She had not to wait long.   In a
few minutes the bedroom door opened,
and Maraquita, leaning on the arm
of the old negress, walked slowly into
the apartment.   She was robed in a
white muslin gown.   Her dark hair was

hanging loose upon her shoulders, and her face was as white as her attire. There was an ethereal look about the girl that naturally excited pity, and the scared expression on her features went straight to Liz's kindly heart. In a moment she had sprung to her assistance.

'You are still very weak, Quita. Are you sure you feel equal to leaving your room?'

'Oh, yes, yes,' replied the girl, in a petulant tone, as if she did not like the subject of her illness alluded to. 'There is nothing the matter with me now, Lizzie. I could have returned home two days ago, if your father would have let me. I really think he is *too* particular.'

'How *can* he be too particular where *you* are concerned,' said Lizzie gravely, as she placed the trembling Quita on the sofa. 'Mr Courtney confided you to his care, and trusted him to look after you as if you were his own child, and father has felt the charge to be a sacred one.'

'He is very good,' replied Maraquita, in a low voice; 'but I have not been so *very* ill, Lizzie, after all, and I am all right again now. I hope nobody will make a fuss about it.'

Liz was silent, for she did not know what to reply. They had reached a point where confidence came to a full stop between them, and she could hardly have spoken without perverting the truth. So she tried to change the subject.

'How soon do you expect Mr and Mrs Courtney to fetch you, Quita?'

'I don't know. I think the Doctor

has walked up to the house to tell them I am ready. Mamma will be surprised to find *you* didn't nurse me, Liz. Why didn't you do so ?' inquired Quita nervously, as if she wanted to find out how much or how little of her secret had been confided to her foster-sister's discretion.

But she had not fathomed the depths of Lizzie's character. She had sworn not to reveal what she knew, and she would have been torn to pieces on the rack without confessing it. It was useless of Quita, or any other person, attempting to force it from her.

'Why didn't I nurse you, Quita ? Not because I was unwilling; you may be sure of that. Simply my father said he did not wish me to do so, and that was enough for me. I have been trained to understand that the first duty of a medical assistant is implicit obedience. I have full faith in my father's discretion, and know that he would not lay one restriction on me that was unnecessary. I can tell you no more than that. Only believe that it was not my own wish, and that if I *might* have nursed you I gladly would.'

'It was best not, or you might have caught the fever. You know that I have had a touch of the fever?' continued Quita interrogatively, but with downcast eyes.

Liz could not answer '*Yes.*'

'I heard my father tell Mr and Mrs Courtney so,' she said, after a pause.

Her reticence alarmed Maraquita. She didn't like Liz's calm, collected manner and short replies.

'Well, I suppose your father doesn't tell lies,' she answered brusquely.

'I have always believed him,' said Liz sadly. 'But, Quita, you have talked enough. Your face is quite flushed. Keep quiet, like a good girl, or you may not be able to return home with your parents, and that will be a great disappointment to them.'

She took up her work again, and commenced sewing, whilst Quita lay still, but with a palpitating heart, as she wondered what Liz could have meant by evading her question. Could she have read her friend's thoughts at that moment, her curiosity would have been satisfied, though not in the way she desired. Liz was marvelling, with a feeling of contempt, as she stitched industriously at her calico, how any woman could bring a child into the world, lawfully or unlawfully, and think only of her safety afterwards, without one thought for her own flesh and blood; the flesh and blood, too, of some one who *ought* to be so much dearer to her than herself. She sat there, nervously anticipating every moment to feel Quita's little hand slip into hers, and to hear her quivering voice ask for news of her child.

Liz would have loved her a thousand times more for the weakness. She would have forgiven her all her frailty and wickedness in one moment, and taken her into her arms with a loving assurance that her infant should be as carefully guarded as the secret of its birth. But no such appeal came from the young mother. On the contrary, she seemed anxious and worried about herself alone, and the only excuse which Liz had been able to conjure up for her sinfulness, grew weaker and weaker with the passing moments. But perhaps, thought Lizzie, with her ever ready charity, perhaps Quita had learned all she wished to know from Dr Fellows, and her own hasty judgment of her was a grievous wrong. But both the girls felt there was a barrier raised between their intercourse that had never been there before, and it was a relief to them to hear the sing-song chant of the palanquin bearers as they came through the grove to fetch Maraquita away.

In another minute Dr Fellows appeared upon the threshold, accompanied by Mr and Mrs Courtney, and Quita was in her parents' arms. In their delight at receiving her again, they almost forgot to ask for any particulars concerning her illness.

'Oh, my dear child!' exclaimed her mother impressively, 'I hope you have thanked Dr Fellows as you should do for all his attention to you. I don't believe anybody could have brought you round so quickly as he has. Your father and I were dining with the Governor, Sir Russell Johnstone, last evening, and he said that Dr Martin of the Fort had told him no cases of fever had been declared convalescent under three weeks. And here you are, you see, almost well again in a third of the time.'

'Not so fast, my dear madam,' interposed the Doctor. 'As you are naturally anxious to have her under your own care, I can pronounce Miss Courtney to be sufficiently recovered to be moved to the White House, but I shall visit her every day, and it will be some weeks before she is completely off the sick list. But she must eat as much as she can, and do as little as she need, and she will soon be strong again.

'But if you think it would be more prudent for her to remain here a little longer under your care, my dear Fellows, we are quite willing to leave her,' said Mr Courtney.

'No, no!' cried Quita, clinging to her mother's neck, and sobbing. 'Take me home, mamma! I am longing to get away, and to be with you.'

'That does not sound very grateful in you, my dear,' said her father, 'considering all that you owe to Dr Fellows, and Lizzie.'

'Don't mention it!' cried the Doctor quickly. 'She is weak, and nervous, and hardly knows what she is saying, and the worst thing in the world for her is this agitation. She will be much better under her mother's care. Take her home at once, Mr Courtney, and let this exciting scene be ended.'

He threw a mantle over Maraquita's shoulders as he spoke, and placed her in the palanquin, which was in the verandah. The bearers raised their burden to their shoulders and set off at a walking pace, the rest of the party keeping by their side.

They had all been so occupied with the removal of Maraquita, that they had hardly noticed Lizzie, who stood at the open window watching their departure. So this was the end of it! The last week had passed like an unholy dream to her,—a dream of which she had had no time to read the import until now. Should she ever unravel it? Would the tangled meshes which it seemed to have woven round her, fall off again to leave her free? She did not see the way to burst her bonds, but she resolved that she must know the worst concerning herself and Henri de Courcelles at once. She felt that it would be impossible for her to live on, and do her duty as it should be done, whilst any moment might bring an exposure to sever her from her lover. She was still pondering on her troubles when Dr Fellows slowly re-entered the bungalow.

'How did she bear the journey?' asked Liz, as she caught sight of her father. 'She seemed to me too weak to attempt it.'

'So she would have been under ordinary circumstances, but of two evils we must choose the least. The poor child's life here was one of torture, from the fear of detection. She will feel safer at the White House, and her recovery will be more rapid in consequence.'

' And meanwhile, she doesn't care one jot if her infant lives or dies,' said Liz contemptuously.

Dr Fellows regarded her with mild surprise.

' You are very hard on her, my daughter. Cannot you make some allowance for the terrible position in which she is placed ? '

' I cannot understand it,' she answered.

' No, and you never will—thank God for it. Your sense of right and wrong is too clear to permit you to be led astray. But this poor child is very different in character from yourself. She is weak, and foolish, and unprincipled,

and the scoundrel who has taken ad-
vantage of her simplicity, should be
strung up at the Fort. It seems a
shame that, in order to protect her
good name, he should be allowed to
go unpunished. But perhaps you cannot understand that also.'

' Father, you mistake me!' cried
Lizzie. ' I can love, or I believe I
can, as fondly as any woman, and I
can well imagine the force of the temptation which circumstances might bring
with it. God forbid that I should
judge any error that springs from too
much love, or consider myself beyond
its reach. But I *cannot* understand the
selfishness that makes a woman shrink
from the consequences of her sin, as
if it had no claim upon her. Where
is the father of this child? If I were
Quita, I would rather go out into the

world with my baby in my arms, and beg from door to door by *his* side, than run away as she has done, and leave it to the care of strangers.'

'Hush, hush!' exclaimed the Doctor quickly, looking round them with a face of fear. 'Even the walls have ears. Remember your oath, Lizzie, and never mention this subject, coupled with her name, again.'

'Let me ask you at least, father, if you have seen Mammy Lila.'

'More than once, Lizzie, and all will be right there, until I have time to decide what is best to be done in the future. But it will be a terrible puzzle, and I must think it over gravely. I am ill and weary at present, and would rather leave things as they are for a month or two.'

'I, too, feel ill and weary,' rejoined Lizzie sadly. 'I have not liked to worry you with my own troubles whilst you were attending on Quita, but now that she is gone, father, I must ask you one question. What am I to do with regard to what you told me on the night that she came here, and you extracted that oath of secrecy from me?'

'Do! What would you do?' demanded Dr Fellows, with a white face.

'I don't know. The knowledge seems to have laid a burden on me too heavy to be borne. Had I only myself to consider, my task would be, comparatively speaking, easy. I could take care that I suffered alone. But there is Monsieur De Courcelles; I must consider him.'

'What has De Courcelles to do with it?'

'Father, how can I contemplate a marriage with him without first telling him the truth? Am I to leave it to chance whether he finds out or no that —that you did what you told me? I could not do it. Such a life would kill me. I will marry no man unless he knows the whole story.'

'Would you betray my confidence?' exclaimed Dr Fellows bitterly. 'Have my long years of secret sorrow and humiliation not been sufficient punishment for me, but that my child will hold me up to public degradation?'

'No, no, father; do not say that! Not a word that you uttered shall ever pass my lips without your free consent. I will do anything rather than repeat them. I will even give up—Henri de Courcelles.'

' And would that break your heart, my dear ? '

' Never mind if it breaks my heart!' she cried, with a sudden storm of weeping; ' if it must be, it must be, and there is no alternative. I love him too well to deceive him, and I love you too well to betray you. It is no one's fault— it is only my misfortune; but I must end it at once and for ever, or it will get the better of me. To-morrow I will tell Henri de Courcelles that our engagement is at an end.'

' Do nothing in a hurry,' replied her father wearily. ' Be patient for a few days, Lizzie, and we may think of some way out of this dilemma. You owe it to Monsieur de Courcelles as well as to yourself—'

At this moment a young negress, with a yellow handkerchief bound about her woolly head, and the tears running down her black cheeks, hastily entered the bungalow.

'Massa Fellows,' she cried, 'I bring berry bad news. Poor Mammy Lila gone to heaven! Mammy took sick with fever last night, and no one to send for Doctor but me, and I got de chile to tend. So Mammy say, "Gib me pepper pot, and I all right to-morrow;" but morning time Mammy go home. And Aunty Cora come and stay by her, and she tell me take dis chile back to Dr Fellows, 'cause Mammy Lila dead, and dis nigger must go home to her fader and moder.'

'Why, it's Judy, Mammy Lila's grand-child, and she has brought the infant back again!' exclaimed Liz, as she saw the bundle in the girl's arms.

'Mammy Lila gone! Here's a misfortune to upset all our plans,' said the Doctor.

'Father, what are we to do?'

'We can do nothing but keep the child here—at all events for a few hours, Liz. I know of no one else to take charge of it, or, at least, no one whom I could trust. To-morrow I will go over to the Fort and consult Dr Martin; but for the present it must remain with you, and I will take this girl back to Shanty Hill, to see that she speaks to no one in the plantation. Here, Judy, give the baby to Miss Liz, and you shall go back to Shanty Hill with me. Are you *sure* that Mammy Lila is gone?'

'Sure, massa! Why, she cold as a stone, and Uncle Josh making her coffin already. The last words she sez was, "Take chile back to Doctor, and say

Mammy can't do no more ;" and den she lay her head down and shut her eyes, and I run for Aunty Cora, and she say Mammy dead as a door nail.'

'All right, Judy. I'm very sorry to hear it, but I'll go back with you all the same.'

He reached down his hat and stick as he spoke, and turned to his daughter before he left the room.

' I'll be back in an hour or two, Liz. Take the child into the inner room, and don't leave the house till I return. I didn't know the fever had reached Shanty Hill. I must see some sanitary precautions carried out there.'

The young negress placed the infant in Lizzie's outstretched arms.

' You'll be glad to get it back again, I guess,' she said slyly, as she deposited it there.

'I'm not so sure of that,' replied Liz, taking no further notice of the remark, as she carried her burden tenderly away.

She placed it on the bed, and carefully unfolded the wrappings round it. She had a natural curiosity to see the little creature born of one so near and dear to her, even though it had no title but to a heritage of shame. And when she saw it, the maternal instinct so strong in the breasts of all good and pure women rose like a fountain in her heart, and overflowed for the poor motherless and fatherless baby thrown so unexpectedly upon her care.

Maraquita's little daughter was a tiny, fragile-looking thing, with large dark eyes and a waxen complexion, and a wistful, solemn expression, as if she were asking the cold world not to spurn her for her parents' fault. The first view of her touched Lizzie deeply. She hardly knew herself why she cried like a child at the sight of those tiny hands and feet, those grave, wondering eyes, and the head of soft, dark hair that nestled against her bosom. But the best feelings of her nature rose to the surface, and her first idea was that she could never part with the child again, but would tend and rear it for Maraquita's sake. But when she confided her wishes to Dr Fellows, he shook his head in dissent.

'It would never do, Lizzie. It would be too great a risk,' he said. 'The child's presence here would excite general curiosity. The talk would reach Maraquita's ears, and its proximity would unsettle her—perhaps cause her to betray herself. There is only one safe course to pursue in these unhappy cases, and that is, complete separation. Take care of the poor little creature to-night for me, and to-morrow I will ride over to the Fort, and see if Dr Martin knows of any trustworthy woman to take charge of it. The regiment is to be relieved next month. If I can get the child shipped off to England, I shall consider it the most fortunate circumstance that could befall it, unless indeed it would die first, which would be still better.'

'Oh, father!' cried Liz reproachfully, as she laid her lips against the baby's velvet cheek.

'It sounds hard, my dear, but it can inherit nothing but a life of shame and loneliness, and it would be very merciful of God to take it. You don't know what it is to live under the crushing sense of shame. Besides, it is a weakly infant, and under any circumstances is not likely to make old bones.'

' I believe that I could rear it, with care and attention,' repeated Liz, wistfully.

' It is impossible,' repeated the Doctor briefly, as he left the room.

But in a few minutes he returned, and walked up to where his daughter was still crooning over the baby.

' Lizzie, I have been thinking over your wish to tell Henri de Courcelles my story. But it must not be, my dear —not at least during my lifetime. You will be angry with me for saying so, but I don't quite trust De Courcelles. We have never got on well together. There is something about him I don't understand. If I should die, Lizzie, and sometimes I think it won't be long, first, you can do as you think fit, but whilst I live, I hold you to your promise of secrecy.'

'And I will keep it,' replied Lizzie, 'as if it had been made to God.'

CHAPTER VII.

MR and Mrs Courtney could not sufficiently express their satisfaction at receiving their daughter back again. Maraquita was their only child. She had never had a brother nor a sister. All their hopes were centred in her, and in their love they naturally exaggerated her beauty, and were blind to her faults. Her father positively idolised her, and her mother's affection, though rather languid and uneffusive, was none the less real. Had Mrs

Courtney exercised a proper *surveillance* over her daughter, Quita could never have suffered the misfortune she had just undergone; but it was not in her indolent Spanish nature to look after anything. She had had a suspicion of Maraquita's condition, but it was only a suspicion, although the old black nurse Jessica had known it for months past. But Jessica had suckled Maraquita from the moment of her birth, and attended on her every hour of the day and night since, and would have died sooner than have brought one word of blame on the head of her young mistress. She had not even let the girl know that she had guessed her terrible secret, and so Maraquita returned to her father's house with as proud a bearing as if she had done nothing to forfeit the esteem of her fellow-creatures, and quite ready to accept all the homage paid to her. She was carried straight from her palanquin to a room redolent of flowers, and laid upon a couch, whilst the household servants ran hither and thither, to bring her refreshment, or to do her service.

Old Jessica was weeping for joy at the foot of her couch to think she had got her young mistress safely back again, and Mr and Mrs Courtney were almost as effusive in their gratitude for their good fortune. Meanwhile Maraquita lay there, lovely and languid, pleased to see how much pleasure she gave them by her recovery, and without a blush of shame to remember how that recovery had been attained. Hers was a frivolous, unthinking nature—easily scared by the approach of danger, but ready to forget everything that was not immediately before her. She was a very common type of our fallen humanity, intensely selfish, and only disturbed by the misfortunes that threatened herself. And now, she believed that she was safe. Her secret was known only to the Doctor, and he had promised her, for her father's sake, that it should never rise up against her. So she reclined there, smiling, with one white hand clasped in that of her father's, and a bunch of orange blossoms—emblems of woman's purity — with which Jessica had presented her, laid against her cheek.

'How lovely our Quita is looking!' exclaimed Mrs Courtney, who was rocking herself in a cane chair opposite, whilst a negress fanned her with a large palm leaf. 'I really think her illness has improved her. She was rather sallow before it. What would Sir Russell Johnstone say if he could see her now.'

'Sir Russell Johnstone,' repeated Quita, whilst Mr Courtney glanced at his wife with a look of warning.

'Yes, dear, the new Governor! Your father and I have seen a good deal of him lately, and he always inquires most particularly after you.'

'Nita, my dear,' interposed Mr Courtney, 'you must not forget that our child is still far from strong, and that Fellows cautioned us against any excitement.'

'I don't believe that pleasurable excitement can hurt any one, Mr Courtney, but if you think it desirable, I will drop the subject.'

'No, no, mother, pray go on. What was it you were going to say? I want

to hear all your news. It seems as if
I had been shut up so long. Tell me
everything you can think of about Sir
Russell, and—and—our other friends.
It will do me good to listen.'

'Sir Russell will have a great deal
to say to you himself by-and-by I expect, Maraquita,' continued her mother,
'and he will want us to take you up
to see Government House. It is such
a beautiful place. You have not seen
half of it at the balls. And the furni-
ture is something superb. It will be
a happy woman who is fortunate enough
to be chosen to reign over it.'

'Is Sir Russell going to marry, then,
mamma?'

'He wishes to do so, Quita.'

'And is the lady in San Diego?'

'He has told your father so, my
dear.'

'Quita,' exclaimed Mr Courtney, as the girl turned her lustrous eyes upon him, 'cannot you guess the truth? Sir Russell Johnstone is almost as eager for your recovery as we are. He has proposed to me for your hand, and he is impatient to have your answer.'

'Sir Russell Johnstone, the Governor of San Diego, wants to marry *me!*' said Maraquita, in a dazed voice.

'Yes, my dear. It is a great honour, but I will not have you biassed,' returned her father. 'You shall do exactly as you like about it.'

'Sir Russell?' repeated Quita, in the same dreamy tone. 'But he is so old, and so ugly.'

'*Old!*' cried Mrs Courtney. 'Why, child, you are raving! He is not a day over forty, and a very good-looking man, although somewhat bald. But that has nothing to do with the matter. It is the position you must look at, and the honour of the thing. Fancy being Lady Russell, and at the head of all the ladies of San Diego, and then going, by - and - by, to live in England, and see all the sights of London, and the Queen, perhaps, and the Royal Family. Why, that chance alone would be worth all the rest, in my estimation!'

'Nita! I won't have our daughter persuaded to do anything against her inclinations.'

'Dear me, Mr Courtney, I am not trying to persuade her! I am only showing her the proper way in which to consider Sir Russell's proposal. Why, he's the highest match in the island, and Quita will never get such another chance if she lives to be a hundred!'

'That's true enough,' replied her husband, 'but she shouldn't marry the Prince of Wales himself, if she hadn't a fancy for him, whilst I have the money to keep her.'

'But stop, father,' interrupted Quita, 'there is no harm in talking it over with mother, and I like to talk of it. It's a great compliment, isn't it? I wonder whatever made Sir Russell think of me?'

'Oh, my dear girl, don't talk such nonsense!' exclaimed Mrs Courtney. 'You *must* know how pretty you are, even if nobody's told you so, and that there's not another woman in San Diego can compare with you. Sir Russell has got a pair of eyes in his head like other men, and he sees you will make the handsomest Governor's lady in the West Indies. And so you will, though it's your mother says it.'

Maraquita was evidently much impressed by the news which had been told her. She lay quiescent on her sofa, but her large eyes were gazing into space, and a faint rose flush had mounted to her face.

'Do you think he is *sure* to take me to England?' she inquired, after a pause.

'Why, naturally, my love, when his three years' term is over here. And he tells me he has a lovely place in the country there, and he's a Member of Parliament into the bargain, and knows all the grandest people in London. Why, you would live like a queen, and be the luckiest woman in the world.'

'And *we* should have to part

with her,' said Mr Courtney, with a
sigh.

'Well, I suppose that would come
some day, in any case,' replied his
wife, 'and there'll be plenty of time
to think of it. Sir Russell has only
been in office six months, and by the
time his term is ended, I don't see
why *we* shouldn't visit England too,
Mr Courtney. You've promised to take
me there, times out of mind.'

'Yes, yes ! unlikelier things have
happened,' said her husband, brighten-
ing up.

'And I should have a splendid wedding,
shouldn't I ?' mused Maraquita.

'You should have the grandest wedding
that's ever been seen in San Diego,'
replied her mother, 'and everybody in
the island, black and white, to see it.
It would be a universal holiday, and

we would send for your wedding dress to Paris, Quita. Monsieur de Courcelles was telling me the other day that—'

But Mrs Courtney was summarily stopped in her recital by a burst of hysterical tears from Maraquita.

'Oh, no! I can't do it; I don't like him enough,' she sobbed. 'He is old and ugly. I *won't* marry him. Don't say any more about it.'

Of course both her parents were full of concern for her agitation.

'I told you how it would be!' exclaimed the father. 'She is far too weak to hear so exciting a topic. You should have held your tongue till she is stronger, and able to decide the matter herself. Don't cry, my dearest child. Try and compose yourself, or I shall be obliged to summon Dr Fellows.'

'You should have more sense,' said

her mother decidedly. 'No one wishes you to do anything that is objectionable to you, Quita. There is nothing to cry for at having a grand proposal made you. However, let us drop the subject for to-day, and perhaps you had better lie down in your own room and have a siesta. Jessica has prepared it for you.'

The two women supported the girl between them to her sleeping-chamber, when Mrs Courtney despatched the black nurse for some iced lemonade.

'Quita,' she whispered, as she lifted her daughter on to the bed, 'you haven't deceived me? There is a mystery about this illness of yours which may ruin your whole life. Take my advice, my dear, and marry Sir Russell Johnstone. It will be your salvation.'

'But, mother,' whispered Maraquita back

again, with her face hidden in her mother's sleeve, ' there—there is *some one else.*'

' Do you suppose I don't know that, and that I needn't go far to find him, either, Quita ? But no woman ever married yet, my dear, without there being "*some one else.*" But he will be no good to you, and you must forget him as soon as you can. You've made a fool of yourself, and your only remedy lies in marriage ; but you can't marry *him.* Your father would never hear of such a thing. He looks high for you, and he has a right to do so. He would as soon consent to your marrying Black Sandie as—as—'

' Hush, mother !' cried Maraquita. ' Don't speak his name : I cannot bear it.'

' He has behaved like a villain to you, my dear, and you ought to despise him

for it. It is only for your sake that I
have not had him turned off the plantation. But if I hold my tongue, you
must promise to think well over the
advantages of Sir Russell's proposal.'

' I will—I will—'

' It is a perfect godsend, and you would
be a fool to reject it. I can't understand
your being so upset over a piece of good
fortune,' said Mrs Courtney, as she bent
over her. ' I hope—I *hope*, Maraquita,
that you won't let this folly interfere
with it.'

She said so meaningly, for she had
not failed to observe the manner in
which the young overseer and Maraquita had looked at each other on the
occasions of Henri de Courcelles' visits
to the White House. Her daughter
flushed slightly, and turned her head
away.

'Of course not,' she answered pettishly. 'But if I did, what of it, mamma? My father says I am not to be biassed in my inclinations, and that means I may choose for myself.'

'So long as you choose an eligible person, Maraquita; but you quite mistake your father if you imagine he will consent to your marriage with any one beneath yourself. He is very particular on that score. You are our only child, and will inherit all his fortune, and you have a right to make a good match. Now, pray, my dear, don't be foolish. All girls have their little fancies, you know, but they learn to get over them, and you must do the same, won't you ?'

'I don't know what you are talking about, mamma,' replied Quita uneasily. 'All I have to think about now, I suppose, is whether I shall marry Sir Russell Johnstone or not.'

'My dear girl, you make me miserable by even suggesting a doubt on the subject. I am sure of one thing,—if you *don't* marry him, you will never cease to reproach yourself, and be ready to die of envy at seeing Mademoiselle Julie Latreille or one of the other San Diego belles in your place.'

'*Julie Latreille!*' cried Maraquita. 'Why, she can't hold a candle to me! Every one said so at the last regimental ball.'

'Of course she can't, dear, and she wouldn't know how to conduct herself as the Governor's lady either. But when a man is disappointed in one direction, he is apt to try and console himself in another. And Sir Russell is *very* much in love with you, Maraquita; I never saw a man more so.'

'Well, he won't expect me to be in love with him, I hope.'

'What a silly thing to say, my dear! If you will only consent to marry him, I'll guarantee that Sir Russell will be satisfied with anything you may choose to give him. Of course, you will be very grateful to him, and kind and affectionate and all that,' continued Mrs Courtney as an afterthought; 'but it is quite unnecessary that any young lady should profess to be in love with her husband. You can leave all that to the men.'

Maraquita sighed, and said nothing. She possessed a very warm temperament, like most people born of a mixture of bloods, and the prospect of being tied to a man for whom she did not care, was most displeasing to her. Her thoughts reverted to another lover, whom a marriage with the Governor would force her to give up, and the tears gathered in her eyes and rolled slowly down her cheeks.

'Come, my dear,' exclaimed her mother hastily, as she watched the signs of her emotion, 'we will drop this subject for to-day, and you must try and go to sleep. In a short time you will see all the advantages of Sir Russell's proposal, and be very grateful for them. But at present you are weak, and must not think too much. I will leave you alone now, and Jessica shall fan you to sleep.'

But it was very little sleep that visited Maraquita's eyes that day, and it was in vain that old Jessica closed the green jalousies over her windows, and brought her cooling drinks, and fanned her incessantly to keep off the flies. Quita's large dark eyes were fixed upon space, whilst she revolved the question in her mind whether she could possibly marry Sir Russell Johnstone, and always came back to the conclusion that it was impossible. When night arrived, her mother was so distressed to find the symptoms of fever strong upon her, that she wanted to send at once for Dr Fellows, but Quita entreated her not to do so.

'Mamma, dear, let me have my own way, and I shall be all right in the morning. Let me sleep quite alone. Jessica fidgets me. She jumps up twenty times in the night to see if I am asleep or want anything, and when she sleeps herself she snores. She is a good old creature, but I'd rather be left to myself.'

'But, Quita, my dear, supposing you should be ill in the night, and no one near you!' exclaimed Mrs Courtney. 'Why, I shouldn't be able to sleep myself for thinking of it. Let *me* sleep in the next room to yours, my darling. The curtain can be drawn over the open door, and you will be as much alone as if it were shut. And I should be within call if you required me.'

'No, no,' replied the girl fretfully. 'That would be worse than having Jessica in my room, for I should never be certain *when* you were coming. I want to be *alone*, mother—really and truly *alone*—and when the darkness falls, I shall sleep soundly.'

'Very well, my dear,' said Mrs Courtney. 'If it is your whim, you shall be indulged in it, but I shall not dare tell your father that I have consented, or he will insist on sitting up with you himself.'

She kissed her daughter then, and professed to leave her for the night, but she whispered to old Jessica that after she had prepared everything that was necessary, she was to lie down on the mat outside the door of Maraquita's chamber, and listen to every sound that issued from it.

The old negress obeyed with alacrity. She possessed the faculty, common to coloured people, of staying awake for hours if necessary, and even of sleeping with one eye open. The inner door of her young mistress's apartment opened on a corridor, paved with marble, but there were two other doors to it which led out to the garden.

Jessica sat down on a white bear-skin mat in the corridor, and listened for a possible summons. The night drew on apace. The lamps were extinguished throughout the White House, and the master and mistress had retired to rest. The coloured servants were sleeping on mats in the verandahs, and everything was hushed in silence, when midnight struck from the large clock over the stables. The old negress's eyes were just about to close in slumber, when she was startled into consciousness again by the fall of a light footstep on the matted bedroom floor. Maraquita had left her bed. Jessica sat up straight and listened. The light step became more palpable. Quita had put on her shoes and stockings, and was passing through the door that led to the plantation. Quick and stealthy as a panther, and almost as noiselessly, old Jessica crept round another way, just in time to see a dark-robed form walking down the path towards the overseer's bungalow.

'I thinking so,' mused the old woman; 'I *sure* dat man at de bottom of it! Curse him! He's stolen away my poor missy's heart, and brought her into all dis trouble, and now she's out of it, she can't rest without him. Ah, if the massa only knew, he'd *kill him.* And *I'll* kill him if he don't let my missy alone. I'll make him drink obeah water and he shall die. My poor little missy to go through all dis trouble for a man who don't care for her no more than he do for Jerusha. If I only tell Jerusha! *Dat* would finish him once and for ever.'

Meanwhile, Maraquita (for it was

indeed she) was making what haste she could towards her lover's home. She felt very weak as she tried to walk, and her limbs trembled under her, but she would not give in, for her reputation was at stake, and what will a woman *not* do to save her good name? Henri de Courcelles' study or room of business was at the back of the bungalow, and he was in the habit of sitting up there late into the night, reading. Well did the poor girl know her way to that room at the back of the house —well did she know her lover's habits and customs—too well, unfortunately, for her own peace of mind. Henri de Courcelles was surprised and delighted — but not startled — when her slight form passed through the open door, and stood before him. He knew that she would come to him as soon as she was able, but he had hardly expected she would have been able to do so so soon. He leapt from his chair and clasped her in his arms.

'Quita, my darling,' he exclaimed, 'you have returned to me at last!'

The girl did not speak, but she clung to his embrace as if she would never leave it.

'You are trembling, my dearest! You were imprudent, perhaps, to risk visiting me so soon. Sit down, and let me lie at your feet and hear all you have to tell me.'

He placed her in the chair from which he had risen, as he spoke, and threw himself on his knees beside her.

'Do you know what I have suffered during your illness?' he exclaimed. 'I thought the suspense would have driven me mad. And then the awful fear lest you should betray yourself. But tell me, Quita, is all danger over? Is our secret safe?'

'Yes!' she answered wearily. 'It is over.'

'Thank Heaven for that! And no one is the wiser.'

'No one except Dr Fellows, of course. I couldn't deceive *him*. But even Liz does not know. No one knows except him—and you and me.'

'And the child, dearest. Where is it?'

The girl gave a sudden gesture of repugnance.

'Don't speak of it: I cannot bear the thought. I am trying so hard to forget everything. And yet, Henri, I *must* speak, for this once only. Dr Fellows has sent it away to some one up the hills, but I shall never be happy till it is out of San Diego. Cannot you manage it for me? Can't you send it away to America or England, so that I may never hear it spoken of again?'

'Perhaps you would like me to drop it in the sea,' he answered gloomily. It cannot be pleasant for a man to hear a woman express nothing but horror of the child she has borne to him.

'I don't know *what* I want,' rejoined Quita sadly, 'only I am so frightened of what may happen. If my father should ever come to hear of it, I think he would *kill* me.'

'No one shall molest you!' exclaimed De Courcelles sternly. 'You are my wife, Quita, and the man who injures you must answer for it to me.'

'Ah, don't talk nonsense!' she said, shrinking a little from him. 'You know, Henri, that I am *not* your wife.'

'But why should you not be so, Maraquita? Why not take the bull by the horns, and let me confess everything to your father?'

'What are you thinking of?' she cried, in a voice of terror. 'You would only bring down his wrath upon my head. He will never consent to my marrying you.'

'Then marry me without his consent, Quita. Surely that should not be distasteful to you, after all that has passed between us. Come, dearest, you love me, do you not? You have so often assured me so. Why not cross with me to Santa Lucia, and we will break the news of our marriage to your parents from there. Say " *Yes*," Maraquita, for the sake of our child,' he whispered.

'It is *impossible!*' she said back again. 'You are asking me to give up my father and mother for you. It would break their hearts. They would never speak to me again.'

'But why not? They are wealthy, and you are their only child. They can enrich any one on whom your happiness may be placed. They would be angry at first, naturally, but they would soon come round, for they could not live without you, Maraquita. A few weeks would see us all together again.'

'You are mistaken, Henri. My father loves me dearly, but his prejudices are very strong. Only to-night, my mother was telling me that he would never countenance my marriage to any one whom he did not consider an equal match to myself.'

'Heavens! Maraquita! Can Mrs Courtney suspect anything?'

'God knows! She has not actually mentioned the subject to me, but her words fell very much like a warning. Perhaps they were so. Perhaps she intended to caution me on my future conduct. She has at anyrate shown me very decidedly that my father expects me to accede to the views he has formed for me.'

De Courcelles turned pale.

'What views?' he stammered. 'Mr Courtney gave me some hints the other day that you were likely to make a grand marriage, but I felt—I *knew*, that it could not be true.'

'But it *is* true, Henri. Sir Russell Johnstone, the Governor of the island, has proposed for me, and my father insists on my accepting him.'

'And you *will?*' cried De Courcelles, in a voice of anguish.

'What am I to do?' asked Maraquita wildly. 'Can I go to my parents and tell them I have disgraced myself? How would that benefit us? I have already told you they would never consent to my marrying *you.* And *this* marriage will, at all events, shelter me from any risk in the future. No one will be able to harm me when I am the Governor's wife.'

'You will do it!' exclaimed Henri de Courcelles fiercely; 'I feel that you *will do it!*'

At that moment he saw the girl in her true colours—selfish, avaricious and worldly - minded, yet, with the insane blindness of passion, he would have wrested her from the hands of his rival, even though his victory bound him to a life-long curse. His Nemesis had already overtaken him. He had seized his prey, but he could not hold it. He had made Maraquita (as he fondly believed) his own. In doing so, he had outraged every law of morality and friendship. He had even thrown over Liz Fellows, whom he knew loved him so purely and truly, and yet his sins had been sinned in vain. Quita no more belonged to him than the plantation of Beauregard did. She was straining at her fetters even now, and before long she would burst them alto-gether, to become the wife of the Governor of San Diego. As the truth struck home to him, De Courcelles' pain turned to anger.

'You cannot! You *dare not !*' he con-tinued. 'You are in my power, Maraquita, and I defy you to throw me over.'

Then her bravado changed to craven fear. She could lie and deceive, and be selfish and ungrateful, this beautiful piece of feminine humanity, but she was a terrible coward, and her lover's Spanish eyes were gleaming on her like two daggers.

'Ah, don't be angry with me, Henri!' she exclaimed pitifully. 'You know how much I love you. Haven't I given you good proof of my affection? Do you think it possible that I could marry any one else of my own free will?'

'Then you will never marry any one else, Maraquita, for you shall not be coerced into it whilst I live. But I don't feel sure of you yet. Will you promise me, if the Governor's suit is pressed more closely upon you, to save yourself by flying with me?'

'I will!—on one condition, Henri.'

'What is it?'

'That you will shelter me from the shame you have brought upon me. *I* dare not do anything in the matter, but you are cleverer than I am, and may manage it without detection. Only get *it* — you know what I mean — sent away from San Diego, or devise some plan by which it can never be brought in judgment against me, and I — I — will do anything you ask me.'

'You give me your solemn word to that effect?'

'My solemn word, Henri,' she answered, with downcast eyes.

'Then it shall be done — if I have to steal it away with my own hands.

But after we are married, surely *then*, Maraquita—' he said wistfully.

'Oh, don't talk of that now!' cried the girl hurriedly. 'It will be time enough to discuss what we shall do, when the time arrives. But I must go now, Henri, or Jessica may miss me. Perhaps you will come up and see me to-morrow.'

'I will come up, without fail, whether they let me see you or not. One kiss, my darling. Remember that I look upon you as *my wife*, and no one shall wrest you from me.'

'*No one* — no one!' she answered feverishly, as she returned his passionate kisses, and almost wished she had the courage to be true to him. Yet as she crept back to her home through the shadowy, moonlit paths — for she would not let De Courcelles accompany her, for fear of being intercepted — she knew she had been lying, and had no more intention of marrying him than before. She had used his entreaties as a means to her own end, and if *that* were accomplished, she would have no hesitation in breaking the promise she had given him. She could always fall back—so she thought—on the duty which she owed her parents, and if the great misfortune of being found out befell her, and the wrath of her father and mother proved too hard to bear, why, Henri de Courcelles was ready and eager to marry her.

Maraquita did not argue with her own conscience in so many words, but such were the thoughts that flitted through her brain as she traversed the slight distance between the overseer's bungalow and the White House, and noiselessly re-entered her chamber. Jessica, who had watched her go and return, never closed her faithful eyes in slumber until she was assured that her young mistress was safely in her bed again, and, for the first time since she had sought it, fast asleep.

CHAPTER VIII.

EANWHILE Lizzie Fellows, unconscious of her lover's infidelity, sat up the livelong night, cradling his deserted infant in her arms. Whilst the members of the White House were wrapped in slumber, and even Maraquita and Henri de Courcelles had gained a temporary relief from their perplexities, and everything was hushed and silent in the Doctor's bungalow, Liz rocked the wailing infant to and fro, or slowly paced up and down the room singing a soft lullaby to try and soothe it. But the puny little creature refused to be comforted. It wanted the warmth and shelter of its mother's bosom, and bleated as pitifully for it as an orphaned lamb standing beside the dead body of the ewe on a bleak hillside. Liz, who had had a great deal of experience with children, tried all her arts to quiet it in vain. The baby was determined she should have no rest that night.

'Poor wee mite,' she whispered, as she laid her cheek against its face, and a natural instinct made it turn its soft lips towards it to find the breast. 'How can she leave you to the care of strangers? How can she sleep in comfort, not knowing if you cry, or are at peace? If you were *mine*, I would die sooner than give up my mother's right to feed and cherish you, yes, even if the world stoned me for it. How I wish I might bring you up for my own little girl — my little tiny Mara-quita!'

How startled we should be sometimes if the wishes we carelessly utter were to be immediately fulfilled! Liz little thought as she crooned over the unconscious baby, that the hour was rapidly approaching when her puzzle would be not how to keep it, but how to get rid of it. Yet so it was.

All that night she walked the room with its little downy head nestled close to her bosom, and its tiny fingers locked round her own. A dozen times she warmed the milk, of which it could only take a few drops, to keep the flickering life in its frail body, and covered it warmly with flannel, to increase the circulation of its blood, although the hot night air permeated the apartment. It was so feeble, that sometimes she almost thought its heart had stopped beating, and uncovered it with a sudden terror. But the infant slept on, although each breath it drew seemed like a wail, until the shadows dispersed, and the glorious West Indian sun rose like a king, and flooded the island with his glory. There seemed to be no dawn to the watcher, or rather it was so momentary, that the night changed as if by magic into day, and the windows of heaven were thrown open suddenly to let the sunlight stream upon the land. It was the waking signal for all life. The big magnolia flowers opened their creamy blossoms as they felt its rays; the trumpet creepers unfolded their leaves; the mimosa spread herself out as though she would bask in the returning light. A hundred scents filled the morning air, and from the grove of trees came many a chirp — first singly and then in twos and threes, as the birds encouraged their mates to rouse themselves, and come forth to pick up the insects before they hid in the long grasses from the noonday heat. From the negro quarters was borne a sort of humming sound, as of a disturbed bee-hive, as the Aunt Sallies and Chloes and Uncle Toms turned out of their beds, and made their toilets in the open air. The morning had broken. It was five o'clock, and in another half-hour the overseer would be amongst them, and accept no excuses if the whole gang were not drawn up in readiness to march down to the cotton fields or the coffee plantation.

Liz sat in her room with the baby

on her knee, listening for the sound
of his mustang's feet. How often had
she been roused from her sleep as
they passed her window, and breathed
a prayer for her lover's safety before
she laid her head on her pillow again
—or watched for him after a night's
vigil, and given him a bright smile
and a wave of her hand as a morning
welcome. But to-day she shrank from
seeing him. A cloud had risen between them, with the knowledge of her
father's secret, which made her afraid
to meet the eyes of the man from
whom she would be, perhaps, but too
soon parted for ever. Besides, were a
look from her to bring him to the open
window, the sacred trust she held in her
arms might be betrayed. Liz blushed
as she wondered what explanation
she could possibly give Henri de

Courcelles of the child's presence there,
and how curious he would become to
learn its parentage, and moved further
from the window as the thought struck
her.

She need not have been afraid. She
heard his palfrey canter by, and caught
a glimpse of his handsome figure as he
rode past the bungalow; but his head
was filled with thoughts of Maraquita,
and how he could accomplish the task
she had set him, and he never even
turned his head in her direction. Liz
sighed as she observed the defalcation.
It was foolish, no doubt, and unworthy
of a sensible woman, for her first wish
had been to avoid him. But who is
sensible in love?

The little child was sleeping soundly
at last, and Liz laid it on the pillows
of her bed, and commenced her morn-

ing toilet. The thought of her father had suddenly struck her. If he was to ride to the Fort that morning and consult Dr Martin about a foster-nurse for the baby, it was time he was roused and went upon his way. The cool hours are soon over in that climate, and when the sun has fairly risen, it is unsafe for any European to ride about, and her father had not looked well of late.

The excitement of Maraquita's illness, and the necessity for concealment, had told on Dr Fellows, and made his face more drawn and haggard than it had been before. And though he had brought much trouble on her, and might prove the cause of her losing what she most cared for, still Lizzie loved him dearly, and pitied more than she blamed him. To live for years under a load of shame and the fear of detection, what greater curse could any human creature be called upon to suffer ?   Liz's own burthen sunk into insignificance beside it.

Her mind reverted to her early days, when she used to wonder why *her* father's hair was grey, whilst that of Maraquita's was brown, or why Mr Courtney played hide - and - seek with them in the plantation, whilst Dr Fellows shook his head and told her such games were only meant for little boys and girls.   Liz understood it now, and felt almost glad to think she could show her sympathy with all he had gone through, even though she had to sacrifice her own future in order to pass it by his side.

Meanwhile Henri de Courcelles had completed his journey, and reined in his steed at the negroes' quarters. The hands were all ready to receive him — the men chiefly dressed in white or striped linen jackets, with dark blue trousers, and the women in print petticoats, and gaily coloured orange or crimson handkerchiefs knotted about their woolly hair. They were a fine-looking set of coolies, all free men, as they were termed by courtesy, but in reality as much slaves as any before the passing of the Abolition Act. They were not all of African blood. Many had come from the East Indies — had been shipped across in hundreds at a time from Calcutta to San Diego, under a promise of higher pay, and less work, than they could obtain in their own country, and had been landed penniless and powerless, to find themselves compelled to take any wages that were offered them, and do any work they were ordered, because they had no means of returning to India. These coolies were not so muscular and capable of hard labour as the Africans, but they were handsomer, both in face and figure. Some of the women had almost perfect features, and were lithe and supple as young roes; but they all bore, more or less, an expression of melancholy. They were not so well able to cast off care, and make the best of the present, as their companions in slavery, but they were more crafty and more desirous of revenge. Amongst them — standing very much to the front, in fact, as if she wished to attract attention — was a young girl of perhaps fifteen — the age of a child in our country, but of a grown woman in hers. She was tall for her nationality, and had a beautifully rounded figure, with tiny hands and feet, and a face fit for a sultan's harem. She was evidently a coquette, and thought much of her personal appearance, for a bunch of white flowers was twined in her long plaits of hair, and a crimson handkerchief was tied across her bosom. In her arms she held an infant of a few months old, a lusty crowing boy, who showed evident signs of having a mixture of white blood in his composition, and of whom his mother seemed inordinately proud. She was standing so close to Henri de Courcelles' horse, that as he dismounted he brushed up against her, and so roughly as almost to knock her infant out of her arms.

'Ah, sahib! take care of the little baby!' she cried warningly.

'Who's that? Jerusha! Then keep your cub out of my way, will you? Now then, my men, are you all ready? March!'

The coolie girl frowned ominously as the overseer addressed her, but she made no answer. Only as the rest of the labourers moved off in single file to the fields, she remained to the last, sulking, as if she had no intention to move.

'Now then, Jerusha!' exclaimed Henri de Courcelles impatiently, as he told off the last negro, and saw her standing there. 'Make haste, will you?' and he cracked the whip he held as he spoke. He seldom used the whip. It was only his insignia of office, and served as a signal for starting, but it sounded differently in Jerusha's ears that morning.

'You dare beat *us* ?' she demanded menacingly.

'I am not going to beat you, but I dare do anything, so don't be a fool,' he replied, half laughing.

'I'm sick,' persisted Jerusha. 'The child kept me up all night. I'm not fit to work. Sahib must let me go back to my hut.'

'I will let you do no such thing,' replied De Courcelles. 'You're only shamming. You're as " fit " as any woman on the plantation, and you must work like the rest. Now, move on, and look sharp about it.'

But Jerusha was obstinate, and had got the bit between her teeth. She considered herself a privileged person, and at one time had been able to do pretty much as she liked with the overseer. But that time was past. He was tired of her, and disposed to treat her, in consequence, a little more harshly than the rest. Jerusha had reckoned without her host when she thought she could give herself airs. When De Courcelles ordered her to move on, she shrugged her shoulders and stood still.

'Now, are you going?' he asked her sharply.

'I telling sahib I'm too sick.'

'And I tell you you're a liar. If you won't move of your own accord, I will make you.' He raised his whip as he spoke, and Jerusha observed the movement.

'You don't *dare* strike me!' she said defiantly; but before the words were well out of her mouth, he had done it, and the long lash curled round her shoulders and stung the baby's cheek, and made the youngster squall. Jerusha's big black eyes flashed fire on him.

'You coward,' she cried, 'to strike your own child! Some day I pay you out for this. Some day *my* whip strike *you.*'

He laughed carelessly at the girl's threat as she joined the gang of labourers, and he flung himself across his palfrey's back, and rode after them. But after a while, when the sun's rays began to beat rather fiercely on his Panama hat, and he found his servant had neglected to fill the straw-covered flask that hung at his saddle bow, he called the yellow girl Rosa and gave the flask to her, and directed her to carry it to the Doctor's bungalow.

'Ask Miss Lizzie to fill it with

fresh sherbet or milk for me, Rosa, and tell her I am coming in to break-fast with her by-and-by.'

The residents in hot climates invari-ably partake of two breakfasts; one a light meal taken at break of day, and the other a more substantial one, which they can discuss at leisure when the morning's business is concluded. Rosa, who was a lazy wench, who preferred running messages, or doing odd jobs, to regular work at any time, ran with alacrity to the Doctor's bungalow, and began to sneak around it. A negro employed on business can very seldom go straight to the matter in hand. He generally slinks about first, peering into windows, and listening at doors, and on this wise it came about that Rosa's cunning face was very soon to be seen at the open window of Liz

Fellows' room. The apartment was empty, Liz having just left it to go to that of her father, but from a bundle of flannel on the bed proceeded a wailing cry, which roused all Rosa's curiosity. The black people are proverbially curious, but this was a case in which the offence might surely be termed a venial one. And with poor Rosa too, who had so lately been bereft of her own child.

As soon as she recognised the cry, she leapt into the room through the window, and rushed up to the bed. Yes! it was actually a baby, and a white baby too, and in Miss Liz's bed! What inference but *one* could be drawn in any ignorant mind from such a circumstance? Miss Liz, who had been so angry with her for the same thing; who had said her poor little Carlo had better never have been born; who had talked so much to her of virtue, and purity, and the sanctity of marriage. Miss Liz had a baby in *her* bed, that she had never told anybody about! Here was a glorious opportunity for revenge. Rosa's eyes rolled about and showed their yellow whites as she thought of it. Miss Liz hadn't pitied her, or so she chose to believe. Why should she pity Miss Liz? And why shouldn't Massa Courcelles, and all the niggers, and the people at the White House, know what she had done? The engagement between Liz and Henri de Courcelles had been kept so secret that no one could say it was a positive fact, but most of the plantation hands knew he had courted the Doctor's daughter, and believed that it would end in marriage. Rosa showed

all her white teeth as she chuckled
over the idea that now perhaps the
overseer would have nothing more to
do with Miss Lizzie, and she would
be pointed at and scorned, as Rosa
had been, when first she appeared
out of doors with little Carlo in her
arms. As the yellow girl thought
thus, she slipped off the bed, where,
she had mounted to better examine the
baby, and left the room as noiselessly
as she had entered it. A cunning
idea had flashed across her brain,—
that if Miss Lizzie caught her there,
she would hide the infant, and no
one would be ever the wiser. So she
must get back to the field without
seeing her, and invent some excuse
for her return, on the way. She was
quite ready with it by the time she
reached the side of De Courcelles,

and she lied so glibly that at first he did not suspect her of an untruth.

'Miss Liz have got no sherbet, Massa! She very sick all night, and drink all de sherbet. But Miss Liz want to see you berry particuler and berry directly, please, Massa. She got something berry important to say; and she tell me,—"Rosa, go and fetch Massa Courcelles here directly, and come back with him all de way."'

'That's a curious message, Rosa. What does Miss Liz want *you* for?' asked De Courcelles, as he turned his steps towards the bungalow, with the yellow girl by his side.

'How can *I* tell Massa Courcelles? P'r'aps Miss Liz want me to mind de baby a bit. P'r'aps she want to ask my 'pinion. Miss Liz know how well I look after my poor little Carlo 'fore de fever come and taken him to heaven.'

The words naturally attracted the overseer's attention.

'*The baby!*' he exclaimed, taken off his guard. 'What do you mean?'

Rosa's cunning eyes looked full into his own.

'You not *know?*' she said inquisitively. 'Miss Liz not tell you she got a little baby at the bungalow—and in her own bed too? Ah, Miss Liz berry sly—but it's truth, Massa. I have seen it with my own eyes. A little white baby, too, only dressed like a little nigger in a cotton shirt.'

'Rosa, you must be dreaming. You are lying to me,' said Henri de Courcelles, suddenly alive to the danger of the girl's discovery. How can Miss Liz have a baby at the bungalow?'

'Ah, Missy Liz knows that best herself,' replied the yellow girl, with an oracular nod; 'but it's God's truth, all de same, Massa, and dere's not much difference 'tween white gal and yaller gal, after all. Miss Liz berry angry with me because little Carlo come a bit too soon, but dere's a baby come to her now, and I shall have my revenge.'

'Don't talk nonsense!' exclaimed De Courcelles; 'and don't presume to speak to me in that way of Miss Liz.'

But though he affected to be angry, he saw a light glimmering through the clouds of perplexity that overshadowed him, all the same. What if this child

—for he could not doubt *which* child
Rosa meant—should be taken by the
plantation hands for Lizzie's? How
fortunately the circumstance would divert
public suspicion from his poor Maraquita! It never occurred to him what
a piece of dastardly cruelty it would be
to shift the blame from one woman
to the other, so selfish does the
madness of passion render us. But
he could not understand how the infant came to be at the bungalow, and
he was painfully curious on the subject.

'Massa Courcelles not believe me?'
continued Rosa, as they drew in sight
of Lizzie's window; 'then Massa just
come here and look for himself.'

The yellow girl was standing before
the open casement, and beckoning to
him as she spoke, and something

stronger than mere curiosity urged him to obey her summons. He drew near on tiptoe, and peeped in. The infant was still lying on the bed, its tiny face uncovered to the air.

De Courcelles was not a man much subject to the softer emotions, but as he looked at it, he trembled. In another moment he had started backwards, for the bedroom door opened, and Lizzie herself appeared upon the threshold, and, taking up the baby, carried it into the outer room.

'Now do you believe I telling lies?' exclaimed Rosa triumphantly, as she looked up into the overseer's pale face; and before he could prevent her, she had run round the house, and in at the front door.

Fearful of what discovery might follow her intrusion, De Courcelles hurried after her, and arrived just in time to see the mock curtsey which she dropped to the Doctor's daughter. Lizzie herself, taken at a disadvantage, and utterly unprepared at that early hour of the morning for visitors, was standing by the table, white as a sheet, holding the baby in her arms, and apparently unable to say a word.

'Good morning, Miss Lizzie!' cried Rosa, with another deep reverence. 'Massa Courcelles and I jest come round to see you and de new baby, and to ask how you both do to-day.'

'What do you mean?' said Lizzie, though she knew well enough, as she stood before them white and trembling.

'Ah, Miss Lizzie, you berry sly.

You know berry well what I mean. I
want to see dat nice baby of yours.
Is he like my little Carlo?   Ah! I
know he's white, like his moder, but
I will love him all de same, if you will
let me.'

'Henri,' said Lizzie, with an assump-
tion of great calmness, in order to cover
the shaking of her voice, 'will you
stand by silent and hear this girl insult
me ?'

'Certainly not,' he replied. 'Go back
to the field, Rosa, and continue your
work. You said Miss Lizzie asked you
to return with me, or you should not
have come.'

'She deceived you,' said Lizzie. 'I
have not seen her nor spoken to her
this morning.'

'I know dat berry well,' cried Rosa
impudently ; 'but I come to see dat

baby of yours, and I bring Massa Courcelles to see it too. And now I will go back to my work with a light heart, for I wish you joy, Miss Lizzie, and I hope de Lord won't send for dat baby of yours same He did for my poor little Carlo,' and with another curtsey, the yellow girl turned on her heel, and ran out of the bungalow, leaving Henri de Courcelles and Lizzie together.

She was the first to speak.

'Had you any knowledge of Rosa's intentions when she brought you here?' she asked quietly.

'Not the slightest, upon my honour,' he replied. 'I sent her to you with my empty flask, to beg a little sherbet, and she returned with a message that you desired to see me at once, and that *she* was to accompany me back again. On the way, she told me a story that I found it almost impossible to believe.'

'And what was the story?'

'That — that — you have a white infant at the bungalow. Is it true?'

'You can see for yourself that it is true! What then?'

'Whose child is it? Where does it come from?' he asked, in a nervous voice, for he fully believed that, being alone, she would confide the secret of Maraquita's shame to him.

But she was silent.

'Why will you not tell me?' he continued, more boldly; 'it is impossible but that you must know. You cannot be sheltering a child of whose origin you are not aware.'

'Why should it be impossible?' she

answered; 'might I not have found it, or adopted it?'

'Nonsense!' he rejoined impatiently; 'where did you find it then?'

Again she was silent.

'Lizzie! I resent this want of confidence between us. Considering how we stand to one another, I have a right to ask you whose child that is. Do you know what Rosa thinks and says about it?'

'It is nothing to me,' returned Lizzie proudly, '*what* Rosa may think or say.'

'But it may be a great deal to *me*. It is not very pleasant for me to hear your name handled and defamed by the black brutes I look after,—to know they speak of you lightly, and say—'

'What do they *dare* to say?' she exclaimed, as she turned and faced him, with the infant on her breast.

'That that infant is your own!'

There was the silence of a minute between them, and then she said, in a low voice,—

'And what do *you* say?'

'That I require to be satisfied who it belongs to, and that you must tell me.'

'*I cannot!*'

There was such an amount of quiet despair in her voice as she pronounced the words, that De Courcelles felt at once that Maraquita's secret was safe, and that she would not disclose it even to *him*. And with the conviction, came a glad, unworthy satisfaction that her guilt and his would be concealed, even at the expense of their most faithful friend.

'*You cannot?*' he repeated, in a voice of feigned astonishment. 'But I say *you must*, or everything shall be over between us!'

'Henri!' she exclaimed earnestly, 'think — think what you are doing. You cannot possibly suspect *me!* Why, I—I—*love you!*' she ended falteringly, as if that confession must clear her at once, and for ever.

'It's all very fine talking,' he answered roughly, 'but facts are ugly things; and if there is any honourable explanation of them, I have a right to demand it. You have a newly-born infant in your arms, and all the plantation is talking of it. If you are not its mother, *who is?*'

Lizzie turned away from him proudly.

'Go and find out for yourself,' she said. 'If you can suspect me even for one moment, you are unworthy of my affection. I will not lower myself to contradict your base suspicion. Think what you will, and act as you think best. I can tell you no more than I have done already.'

'Then I am to believe Rosa's story?'

'You can believe what you choose. This child was given in trust to me by my father, and I am not at liberty to speak to you, or any one, concerning it. It is by an unhappy accident that it has even been seen. I cannot remedy that, but I can prevent the mischief going further. If you cannot accept my word that it bears no relationship to myself, I can do no more than deny it. On any other subject, my lips are sealed.'

Admiration for her sisterly devotion and fidelity had almost made him forget the part he had to play; but the thought of Maraquita came to his assistance, and nerved him to complete his cruel task.

'Well, I will not court your confidence further, Lizzie,' he said, rising, 'but you must consider our engagement at an end. It would be impossible to be happy in married life with a secret like this between us. You *may* have told me the truth, but I am not convinced of it; and where there is distrust, there can be no love. Let us part now, and for ever.'

For the first time, the extent of the sacrifice she was making seemed to strike Lizzie's mind.

'No! no!' she screamed, rushing

after him; 'I cannot part with you thus! Oh, Henri! think a moment! Think how I have loved you! Can you imagine it possible that I should have been so false to you — so false to myself? I swear to you on my knees, and before God, that this child is not mine. Will not that content you?'

'No! nothing will content me now —not even if you attempted to cast the blame on some one else. You have spoken too late, Lizzie. Nothing but conscious guilt would have kept your lips closed until this moment.'

'You shall *not* believe it of me!' she exclaimed vehemently. 'I will not throw my good name away so recklessly. My father is sleeping still. He has been ill and weary lately, and I thought it kind to let him rest; but he would never forgive me for letting him sleep on whilst his daughter's fair fame was being called in question. Stay but one moment, Henri, and my father shall tell you that I speak the truth.'

She flew past him to the Doctor's sleeping apartment as she spoke, and Henri de Courcelles, anxious to know the best or worst at once, stood where she had left him, gazing after her retreating form.

But in another moment a piercing cry of agony sent him to her side. He found her standing by the bed, staring at her father's still, cold features.

'He is gone!' she exclaimed wildly. 'See here, Henri, he is dead—*dead*, and can never now release me from my oath! O God! have pity on me!'

And with that she fell to weeping over the prostrate form.

'*Dead!*' echoed De Courcelles, momentarily awed into the reverence we all feel at the approach of the White King. 'But now, at least, you are free to tell me the truth, Lizzie.'

'Never!' she cried. 'My lips are sealed as his own for evermore. If I could keep my vow to the living, how much more do you suppose will I hold it sacred to the dead? Act as you think right, Henri, but I will never tell you the name of the mother of this child.'

'Then all is over between us,' he returned, as he slunk away, heartily ashamed of himself, and yet with a load lifted from his breast as he remembered that he had unconsciously, but surely, obeyed Maraquita's behest, and might boldly claim the reward she had promised for it.

END OF VOL. I.

COLSTON AND COMPANY, PRINTERS, EDINBURGH.

www.ingramcontent.com/pod-product-compliance
Lightning Source LLC
Chambersburg PA
CBHW030806020726
47499CB00006B/1793